I0657675

Sunken Dreams

A Mark Daniels Mystery

Sunken Dreams

A Mark Daniels Mystery

Justin Maxwell

ABSOLUTELY AMAZING eBOOKS

ABSOLUTELY AMAZING eBOOKS

Published by Whiz Bang LLC, 926 Truman Avenue, Key West, Florida 33040, USA.

For information contact:
Publisher@AbsolutelyAmazingEbooks.com

ISBN-13: 978-1945772702 (Absolutely Amazing Ebooks)

ISBN-10: 1945772700

Karen

Sunken Dreams

A Mark Daniels Mystery

Chapter 1

1735 - Sueños de ángelos (Dreams of Angels)

The cargo was loaded, the lateen sails were raised and the lines cast off. Slowly the *Sueños de ángelos* drifted on the wind away from the wharf at La Habana Harbor.

Capitán Giovanni Andrea de Bazan, master of the ship stood at the forecastle as the 100-foot galleon began its voyage back home, back to Spain. The ship's manifest recorded a cargo of passengers, spices, tobacco, sugar, and other agricultural products from the Spanish territories in the New World. Since they were a merchant ship not a treasure ship transporting gold, silver and gems, they didn't carry much in the way of armament. Neither did the ship sail in a fleet with gunships to protect them from pirates. The *Sueños de ángelos* sailed alone.

Once free of La Habana Harbor, the crew climbed to the yards and unfurled the square sails and the capitán set a course that would take them between La Florida and the isle of Cuba. There the Gulf Stream current would carry the ship back to Spain. The capitán was well aware of the hazards that could befall his ship; pirates stalked the waters of the Caribbean and preyed on Spanish ships and there were often storms on the route that grew to tremendous proportions. Just years earlier a 28 ship fleet was overcome by a hurricane and two of the galleons filled with gold, silver and other riches were overcome and lost to the sea.

With a full set of sails; seven square on three masts, six lateen high in the rigging and another on the bowsprit, the ship sailed on the calm seas and a light wind along the dangerous coral reef of the Los Martires (Florida Keys).

The following day the crew awoke to a dark and ominous eastern sky. Capitán Andrea de Bazan ordered a more northerly course hoping to steer away from the storm. The course change came too late and the storm quickly bore down on the Sueños de ángelos. Before he could give the order to strike the sails the wind gusted, lightning filled the sky and the waves grew immense. A man climbing the shrouds now would surely be blown to his death. As the tremendous storm bore down on the ship, the sails one by one were shredded by the incredible wind until all that remained were tattered fragments. The mizzen mast broke under the onslaught of nature and fell to the deck, crushing two sailors. The helmsman and the mate hugged the whipstaff trying to keep the ship into the wind until it suddenly slackened when the stern post broke. There was nothing captain and crew could do, the sails were gone and the stern post broken; the Sueños de ángelos was without steerage, the passengers, crew and Capitán Giovanni Andrea de Bazan were at the mercy of the wind and placed themselves in the hands of God.

The ship violently pitched and rolled in the seas and was blown miles back west, until the Sueños de ángelos was forced on to the coral reef off the Los Martires, the ship ground to a halt. Passengers aboard cheered, their prayers had been answered, they would not die a death by drowning in the depths of the Straits of Florida. But the capitán knew their lives were still in peril. The ship was grounded on a shallow coral reef in a hurricane and would be beaten by the waves and pounded into the reef.

Several sailors tried to launch the yawl but the intensity of the hurricane catapulted it end over end in the wild surf, throwing its crew to certain death.

The sounds were deafening; the wind exceeding 130 miles per hour was howling through the rigging, the roar of the huge waves pounding down on the reef, lightning, followed by tremendous crashes of thunder, illuminated the horror of the wood hull of the Sueños de ángelos being smashed on the coral reef.

Capitán Giovanni Andrea de Bazan sat in the stern castle protecting the cargo that was not recorded on the ship's manifest, not reported to Spanish authorities, his eleven chests of silver coins. It was his personal treasure from the Spanish Territories, a fortune he did not want to share with the king. He bought the coins from an old man who said they had been in his family for many years. The man wasn't able to sell them to a treasure ship because his father worked at the mint and stole them one at a time until he had amassed a fortune in silver coins. Some of the coins were newly minted and others very old.

The Capitán couldn't protect his illegal fortune from the ravages of nature but he could protect it from his thieving crew. He knew that in the teeth of the storm, as death loomed close, the crew would try to steal his treasure, so they could at least die rich men.

But they would have to steal it over his dead body. The Capitán sat on a chest, rocking side to side as the Sueños de ángelos was pounded by the waves. He held on with one hand and in his other hand he held a musket.

For 14 hours Sueños de ángelos was viciously pounded on the reef as the ship broke to pieces. Passengers and crew were washed into the boiling ocean and died when their bodies were smashed into the jagged coral or were drowned in the pounding surf. There were no survivors. Some of the crates of tobacco, spices, and sugar washed up on Cayo de Bacas, to be salvaged by the Calusa tribe. The chests of coins that Capitán Giovanni Andrea de Bazan had smuggled aboard, the riches he dreamed would make his family respected by the aristocratic elite, the silver he dreamed would finance more trips to the new territories, sank to the reef. Some chests broke open on impact spilling their riches, the coins fluttered on the current while other chests lay intact, housing their cargo of silver coins stolen from the King.

After the destruction of the ship, there was no attempt to salvage the eleven chests of silver coins; no one living knew of their existence. The records in Havana listed the Sueños de ángelos as a merchant ship carrying agricultural products not treasure. The heavy wood chests settled to the reef and sat there through the centuries. Eventually the wood of the chests was devoured by shipworms and decay, the cargo of silver coins became oxidized by the salt water and lay in black, encrusted, congealed masses. Over the centuries storms washed some of the riches off the reef into deeper water and some of the treasure tumbled with the waves along the sandy bottom towards shore, alternately being covered and uncovered by sand. The treasure of the Sueños de ángelos remained on the bottom of the Atlantic Ocean for almost 200 years.

Chapter 2

In 1931, brothers Charles & Ferran Russel were repairing the 14-foot wood rowboat their grandmother had given them. It belonged to their late grandfather, and Nana decided they should have it. The boys spent hours repairing the old wood boat. They replaced planks that had rotted in the harsh tropical climate of the Florida Keys. And they strengthened the transom just in case they got enough money to buy one of those gasoline motors Mr. Evinrude was selling.

As the twins painted their boat, they told their grandmother of all the fish they would catch, crabs and shrimp they would trap and how they planned to sell them to the restaurants and earn enough to buy a gasoline engine and then save for a bigger boat so they could be commercial fishermen like their father and grandfather. She just smiled and said, "You boys are such day dreamers." They finished painting the hull blue and on the transom they painted; *Day Dreamer*.

On a late August day, the brothers were out on the maiden voyage of their own vessel. They took turns rowing on the waters of Hawks Channel, passing East Washerwoman Shoal out to their father's favorite fishing hole at Delta Shoal near the Sombrero Key Lighthouse.

Just beyond the shallow water of the shoal the bottom dropped off to hundreds of feet in depth. Their father explained to them that nutrients were brought up from the depths and attract small fish ... larger fish come up from deep water to feed on the smaller fish.

They threw out the anchor on the reef in 9 feet of water and the offshore breeze carried them over the area where the bottom dropped off and where the fish were.

The fishing wasn't as good as they had hoped for that day. They thought of staying longer but there was a dark cloud forming to the west and they knew they needed to get in before it got closer. Ferran sat at the oars as Charles began to pull on the anchor line. The boat slowly inched forward until the line was vertical, but the anchor didn't come up, it was stuck in the coral. Try as he might, Charles could not release the anchor's hold. Since they only had one anchor and no money for a new one, cutting the line was not an option.

Charles said, "I'll dive down and see what it's hung up on." He took off his shirt and kicked off his shoes before slipping over the side. Treading water at the bow of *Day Dreamer,* he took a few deep breaths and blew them out then inhaled deeply and dove below. The salt water stung his eyes at first as he kicked and pulled to the bottom.

Ferran watched his brother on the bottom through the clear water. Charles moved rocks away from the anchor then came to the surface for air. He held onto the boat and handed his brother a strange rock he found on the bottom. It was a blackish, encrusted rock. Ferran turned it over in his hand and instantly knew what it was. "It's treasure!" he shouted.

The brothers had seen the silver coins their uncle found on Sombrero Beach a few years back. His black corroded clump contained eight silver Spanish coins, the clump Charles brought up had at least fifty. "Are there any more?"

"Yeah, there are a bunch of them, some even bigger!" Charles said excitedly.

"We gotta get em before the storm gets here cause its gonna wash them off the reef into the deep. Go get 'em!"

The twins were rowing in excitedly discussing how they were going to spend their treasure. They would build Nana a new house and they would buy a new boat with a gasoline engine and they talked about becoming commercial fishermen. The boys kept looking at the large pile of black rocks, showing the distinctive shape of coins, laying on the floorboards of *Day Dreamer*. Ferran asked, "I wonder if it's from a pirate's ship?" Charles just kept repeating, "We're rich, we're rich!"

The storm was rolling in as the boys passed East Washerwoman Shoal; the wind increased and the waves grew. They watched as the sky turned dark gray accompanied by a heavy downpour and the frequent bolts of lightning were followed by deafening thunder. They still had another mile to go.

The wind blew the rain horizontal and the waves were immense. *Day dreamer* was no match for the seas. The boat rose on the waves and dropped into the trough as the boys sat next to one another each pulling on an oar, the rain blowing at over thirty miles an hour stung their faces. They were concerned for their safety and their boat, but mostly they were concerned they would lose their treasure. The harder they rowed towards shore the more the wind drove them away from it. Ferran pulled hard as Charles dragged his oar as a rudder trying to bring the bow back around toward Boot Key. But it also brought the 14-foot *Day Dreamer* abreast of the waves. The boat with its heavy cargo of riches violently rolled from side to side in the trough of the sea. Waves were breaking over the side and the boat was taking on water. As water washed in, the heavily laden boat sat lower. The boys knew their boat was in jeopardy of sinking and taking their treasure with it.

As they struggled at the oars, a large wave crashed down on the boat, flipping it over. The boys, their fishing gear and the treasure were all thrown into the sea. The brothers came to the surface gasping for air and frantically treading water in the angry sea. The thought of the treasure no longer first in their mind, now they were fighting for their lives. Charles frantically grabbed for a board floating nearby; a seat from *Day Dreamer* and he clung to it for dear life as he kicked towards his brother. Through the sheets of windblown rain, they could barely make out the mangroves on Boot Key and kicked towards them.

The twins spent the rest of their lives searching for the treasure of silver that was in their grasp but was snatched away by Mother Nature. They never found it again. Countless storms and hurricanes covered and uncovered the valuable black rocks on the sandy bottom. The tale of a fortune in silver discovered by two brothers in 1931 off Boot Key became a local legend; the legend of the "Twin's Treasure."

Chapter 3

Chago Vasquez climbed up while his wife Riley steadied the rickety homemade ladder. He climbed over the gunnel of the boat and yelled down, "Riley, this looks better than the pictures."

The boat, *Nautical Dreams*, was sitting on blocks in the storage yard at the Southern Star Marina on Crawl Key in the middle Florida Keys. *Nautical Dreams* had been sitting in the same position in the yard for nearly a decade. The owner had the 36-foot wood hull Chris Craft cruiser hauled out for maintenance and he never returned.

Riley stepped back to get a good look at the old wood boat. *Nautical Dreams* sat exposed to the sun, salt air, and the ravages of the tropical storms and hurricanes that assaulted the Florida Keys. The white paint of the hull was peeling so badly it looked like snow on the ground around the vessel. One cabin window was missing, not broken but entirely missing, while the tattered remains of a curtain fluttered in the breeze. An old frayed dock line was hanging off the stern and disappeared in the knee-high weeds. On the transom the name *Nautical Dreams* was faded but legible, although someone had crossed out *Nautical* with a black marker and written above it "*Wet*".

Riley didn't share in her husband's appreciation for the old vessel. In fact, she didn't share in his enthusiasm of living on a boat in Boot Key Harbor either.

"Ya know for an older wooden boat she has held up well," Manny, the marina manager/mechanic/sales manager said. "I think it will serve you good for what you want to use it for. She's a sturdy old boat."

Riley with a skeptical look on her face asked Manny, "The Craigslist ad said the boat has to be moved from the marina by August 28 and that's like in six days. Can we extend that so we can get it ready to live on?"

"No, I've got to get it out of the marina to make way for a boat storage rack the owner wants to build. He wants it out, like yesterday."

"Honey, come up. You gotta see this, it's perfect!" Chago yelled, sitting on the ripped vinyl helm seat.

Manny held the ladder as Riley crawled up and she could feel him watching her ass with each step. She stopped before climbing aboard and took in *Nautical Dreams* in all its glory. The once bright teak woodwork was gray with no vestiges of varnish, the vinyl seats in the cockpit were faded, ripped, or missing and would need to be replaced, the wood companionway door to the cabin hung askew from one hinge and its glass window laid on the deck shattered in pieces. The surface of the deck was mostly bare wood, the paint had vanished long ago, and there was dirt piled in the corners where vegetation grew. Riley's first impression was that the boat was best left on the land to die a slow death rather than launch it and watch the once proud vessel sink to the bottom.

"Come aboard," Chago urged his wife of three months. "Come on, jump in. It's great, it's perfect. We could work on it and get it all fixed up. Come on, jump in."

Riley looked at the deck and wondered if she did jump into the boat if she would break through the wood deck. She slowly climbed over the side and stepped onto the cockpit cautiously testing its strength under her weight.

Riley was startled when Manny asked, "So what do you think?" She didn't know he followed her up the ladder and was standing close behind her.

"I don't know; it looks like it's in pretty bad shape. Do you think it will float?" she asked.

"Oh, sure it will float. When we pulled out the engines I had the guys seal up all the holes. Sure, it'll float," Manny said with the confidence of a man who wasn't going to be the one onboard when *Nautical Dreams* was lowered into the water.

As Chago was exploring the cabin Riley asked Manny, "Why did you take out the engines?"

"The owner hired us to do some work on the boat but he never paid for it, in fact we never saw him again. Anyway, he owed us a bunch of money so we sold off the engines and some other gear. Now since we already covered our expenses we figured we would give the boat away. Ya know, help out someone else. Sort of paying it forward, like they say."

Manny continued, "You're looking for a boat you can live on, not a boat to take a cruise on and this is perfect for what you need. Just anchor it in the harbor and it's your floating house. And it's free! How can it get any better than that?"

Riley warily looked at the helm station and said, "There isn't a steering wheel."

Manny quickly said, "Ya don't need one, no engines, remember?"

Riley went below in the cabin to join Chago.

"Look Riley, we can sleep back here," Chago said pointing to the aft cabin.

Riley looked in the cabin. The built in cabinets on either side of the berth were missing two drawers and two other drawers were broken, and there wasn't a mattress. "What about that missing window?" Riley asked.

Manny responded, "Most people just cut a piece of Plexiglass to fit and you're all set. I think I have some Plexi I can give you."

Chago listening said, "Yeah, we can just put a piece of Plexiglass over the hole, that's how it's done."

"Is that mold?" Riley asked pointing into the bathroom.

"Yeah," Manny said, "There is always mold on a boat, especially in the head. All ya gotta do is wash it with a little bleach and it's gone. No problem."

"Yeah, bleach, no problem," Chago repeated.

Riley walked to the galley where Chago was beaming with excitement as he explored the vessel. "What ya think? She's great, isn't she. We can fix it up and live on her. It will be so cool, just you me and Conchita. I can set up my easel on the back deck and paint. Man it will be so cool. And it's free. It's a free house. We can live on the water and we can save from your teaching salary to fix it up. It's going to be so cool."

Riley could see that Chago was looking at the boat through his artist eye not taking a critical and objective view of what was before him. Riley on the other hand was the more pragmatic, logical and cautious of the two. She wasn't sure that the boat was best for them, and she wasn't sure she wanted to live on a boat in the first place.

"I don't know, Chago," Riley said, "it's in pretty bad shape, and I don't know if we can get it ready in six days."

Sensing the couple might turn down the free boat, Manny said, "That's okay. I have someone else coming later today to take a second look at the boat. It was nice meeting you folks."

"Hold on," Chago said. "Manny, give us a minute to talk about it."

Manny smiled and agreed saying, "I'll be in my truck; I've got to make a call." Manny didn't really have another couple interested in the boat, in fact this was the first anyone had responded to his Craigslist ad for the free boat. If Riley and Chago took the boat, then it would save the marina thousands of dollars. They wouldn't have to pay for the old boat to be disposed of and they wouldn't have to pay the State of Florida abandoned and derelict vessel fees.

Chapter 4

Riley and Chago quickly got a coat of paint on the hull. There was no time to scrape off the old before applying the new, but then most of the old paint had peeled away anyway. By the end of the second day of work on their new floating home, the hull and most of the deck was a glossy bright yellow. Chago found two gallons of paint on the clearance shelf at the hardware store. It was house paint and he figured it should work; after all, *Nautical Dreams* was going to be their house.

After the marina closed for the day, Paulo, an employee at the marina, helped Chago get the mattress off the roof of Riley's car and into the boat. Once in they found the mattress was wider than the berth and had to be curled up on both sides. "Well, we won't roll out of bed anyway," Chago said.

Riley found curtains at the Salvation Army store that almost fit the windows and some cushions. The cushions were for a lounge chair but they nearly fit the bench seat in the galley. The wood of the bulkhead between the aft cabin and the main salon had rotted from years of rain water collecting in the boat so Chago nailed on a piece of wood from a shipping pallet to cover it. Riley and Chago worked to ready their home as their kitten, Conchita, explored and chased mice out from the galley cabinets.

~ ~ ~

The morning of August 28, the deadline to have the boat out of the marina, Chago and Paulo finished installing a marine toilet in the head. All their clothes and the rest of their worldly belongings were tossed on the forward V-berth. Riley surveyed their new home and wondered if they were making a mistake, but they had signed all the paperwork, *Nautical Dreams* was theirs. There was no turning back.

Riley's dad loaned them money to get the boat ready and insisted they get insurance on the boat just in case. He didn't like his only daughter's choice of a husband, but knew he couldn't do anything about her falling in love with an artist whose feet were not solidly rooted on terra firma.

Nautical Dreams strained and creaked as it was slowly lifted off its cradle. Riley watched with a troubled look, Chago was wide eyed with excitement, Manny was smiling because he was getting rid of a liability and Paulo looked intense operating the boatlift, knowing the battered old boat might break in half as he lifted it.

Paulo walked around the boat checking for any problems; any seams that might have separated, anything that would allow sea water in. Chago climbed aboard the boat with a big smile, Riley chewed a fingernail and Manny yelled to Paulo, "Okay, let's get this old girl wet!"

Paulo made the sign of the cross and said a silent prayer to Brendan the Navigator, the patron saint of seafarers. "Please, no let sink," Paulo said as he pushed the joystick forward, motors revved, pulleys turned, cables raised and the yellow wood boat gradually was lifted. Paulo slowly moved the Travel Lift carrying the boat out over the water. The lift stopped and *Nautical Dreams* swung in the straps before Paulo pulled the joystick back and the boat began a slow descent into the waters of the Atlantic Ocean.

Manny watched and smiled, knowing the marina owner would be happy he got rid of the rotting hulk for nothing. Riley watched with tightly clenched fists and held her breath and Paulo prayed as *Nautical Dreams* was gently placed in the water. Chago, onboard for the launch, ran below and looked for water seeping in.

He came up all smiles holding his thumbs up. "She floats! She Floats!"

"Alright!" Manny said, then reminded Chago that the boat had to be gone from the marina by five o'clock.

Feeling sorry for the young couple and being a bit infatuated with Riley, Paulo offered to tow *Nautical Dreams* from the marina to the mooring field in Boot Key harbor.

Paulo, at the helm of his boat, *Zahara*, named after his mother, slowly pulled forward taking the slack out of the tow line. Chago hugged the makeshift rudder he and Paulo fashioned out of a scrap 2x4, a piece of ½ inch plywood and a rusty section of pipe while Riley stood on the bow of *Nautical Dreams* wishing she wasn't part of this.

Paulo cautiously pulled *Nautical Dreams* clear of the other boats at the Southern Star Marina dock, some of which were worth hundreds of thousands of dollars more than Chago and Riley's new house.

The trip from the marina to Boot Key Harbor was about 11 miles. Paulo towed the boat due south through the channel to deeper water then turned to the west along the coast of the Keys. Paulo stood at the helm, checking the depth sounder and slowly towing the big yellow boat. Chago stood at the stern of *Nautical Dreams*, beaming as the captain of his own boat and Riley couldn't get the Beatles song *Yellow Submarine* out of her mind.

Below West Sister Rock just off Boot Key, Paulo checked. They were in 30 feet of water as he watched a couple of jet skis off his port to make sure they didn't cut between him and his tow.

"Isn't this cool!" Chago said to his wife. "I can't believe we are actually doing this. Man this is so cool. Aw shit, we forgot to christen the boat. I was going to have you christen it before we left the dock. It's good luck to christen a boat at its launch. Oh well, we can do it now. Go down below and get a bottle of beer and you can pour it on the bow as a christening."

Riley stepped down the two steps into the cabin and screamed, "Chago! There is water down here!"

"It's okay, all boats have a little water in them," Chago said. "That's why Paulo and I installed a bilge pump."

"No, this isn't a little water, it's a lot of water!" Riley yelled. "A lot of water!"

Chago left the 2x4 tiller and ran to the companionway door, looked down at 3 to 4 inches of water slushing around and yelled, "Fuck! We're sinking! Riley we're sinking!"

Chago looked forward towards the towboat and yelled, "Paulo, we're sinking!"

Paulo looked straight ahead not hearing Chago above the old outboard engine on his boat.

"Paulo! Paulo!" Riley screamed trying to get his attention.

Chago ran down in the cabin looking for something to get Paulo's attention. Wading through the water he found the cooler floating. He pulled out two apples Riley had packed and ran up to the bow where Riley was waving frantically and screaming to Paulo. Chago threw an apple at Paulo's boat to get his attention. It fell short of its mark. The second apple had the distance. Paulo was startled to see an apple land in his boat. He watched it roll around on the floorboards and wondered where it came from. He turned back towards his tow and saw Riley on the bow of *Nautical Dreams* yelling and waving her arms.

Paulo backed off on the throttle.

"We're sinking!" Chago yelled. "There is water in the boat. We're sinking!"

As the boat slowed, Paulo could see *Nautical Dreams* was sitting low in the water. It had taken on a lot of water.

Paulo turned to his stern and untied the tow line, throwing it clear of his propeller, then maneuvered his boat next to the old yellow vessel. He leaned over enough to see the water in the cabin and said, "Your boat be sinking."

Chago shouted for Riley to jump into Paulo's boat. But she yelled back, "I can't find Conchita. I'm not leaving without Conchita."

Chago yelled to Riley, "Get into Paulo's boat and I'll look for the cat." He went below and waded through the water that was rising quickly. It was almost up to his knees. "Conchita!" he yelled. "Come on cat where the hell are you." Thinking how Conchita would find the smallest place and hide from them, Chago feared the boat would sink before he found the kitten.

Chago dug through the pile of clothes on the forward berth, throwing them wildly in search of the cat when he heard a faint meow. He turned around and saw the frightened kitten sitting on a shelf high above the toilet. Chago grabbed the feline, rushed to the cockpit and jumped into Paulo's boat.

He handed Riley the cat, his arms scratched and bleeding from the terrified animal.

Paulo backed away from the sinking yellow boat and pressed the MOB button on his GPS. The Man Over Board button instantly recorded their exact latitude and longitude.

With no engines at the stern to counteract the weight of the water in the bow, the stern rose up as the bow went down. *Nautical Dreams* slowly and unceremoniously slipped below the surface.

The old wood boat with its fresh coat of yellow paint sunk bow first towards the sandy bottom thirty feet below. The bow plowed into the bottom and dug a trench creating a cloud of silt as Chago's dream and Riley's nightmare settled on the bottom.

At the surface, Paulo and Chago were picking up pieces of yellow wood and other debris that floated to the surface as the Monroe County Sheriff's Department Marine Division boat arrived.

Chapter 5

Luckily at the insistence of Riley's father, the young couple had taken out insurance on *Nautical Dreams*. After making only one premium payment, the insurance company was liable for the cost of retrieving the wreck from the bottom of the ocean and cleaning up any environmental contamination.

The insurance company hired Sunshine Marine Salvage to clean up the mess that now lay almost 30 feet below the surface of Hawks Channel in the Atlantic Ocean. The salvage company towed out a 25 by 40-foot barge carrying a 320FL Caterpillar excavator and anchored at the site, about a mile south of Boot Key.

Fortunately, the boat did not have an engine so there was no oil to contaminate the water and any gasoline in the tanks had evaporated years ago, so there weren't any environmental hazards. The bottom was sandy so no sea grass or coral was disturbed and the boat was in deep enough water that it did not pose a hazard to navigation. But the law said it had to be removed.

Divers from Sunshine Marine Salvage would fit rubber inflatable bladders in *Nautical Dreams* and pump air into them from a compressor on the barge. The air filled bladders would raise the vessel up enough for the divers to get 4-inch-wide nylon straps under the hull, then attach the straps to a shackle connected to the excavator's boom. If all went as planned, the hull of the sunken vessel would be lifted to the surface and placed onto the barge. Then the divers would gather all of the smaller remains and put them on a 6 x 8 foot expanded metal frame that the excavator would lift to the barge.

Diver Enrique Fuentes hovered a few feet from the hull waiting for the bladders to raise the boat then in the near blindness of the silted water, he passed the end of the strap under the hull to his father Luis waiting on the port side. Once the strap was snugged up against the hull, the divers swam up and felt their way through the clouded water until they found the 10-inch shackle of the excavator. Then they went back down to the sandy bottom to feed a second strap under the hull.

Everything went as planned and the yellow hull was slowly lifted from the bottom. As the hulk broke the surface the excavator operator, Chopper Wirsbinski, stopped its ascent. He looked, making sure the load was secure and allowed sea water to pour out lightening the vessel, then he slowly raised the yellow hull, setting it carefully onto the barge.

Enrique and his father swam to the workboat, climbed up the stern ladder and shed their scuba gear. They needed to wait for the silt to settle and the visibility to improve before they could go back down and collect the smaller pieces of the wreck. Luis opened a cooler, handed Enrique a can of Presidente and a Medianoche sandwich. The guys had picked up the roast pork, ham, and Swiss cheese sandwiches that morning at the Marathon Cuban Café.

When they finished their sandwiches and the six cans of beer, Enrique laid back against the gunnel of the boat with a flotation cushion behind his back and his cap pulled down over his eyes. He was almost asleep when Chopper yelled from the barge; "Get your lazy asses back in the water. I don't pay ya to sleep!"

The divers put their equipment back on and got back in the water. The visibility was still obscured but they could see enough to gather the remaining wreckage.

Luis swam down to the bottom while Enrique guided the expanded metal platform down. Together they grabbed the larger sections of the boat and swam them to the platform. With each piece picked up and with every kick of their fins, they stirred up the sand lessening the visibility. As the guys lifted a waterlogged seat cushion from the bottom, Luis noticed black rocks that had been uncovered by *Nautical Dreams* impacting the bottom. Even in the cloudy water Luis knew what they were. He had been searching for them since he first came to America 32 years earlier. It was his dream to find the black rocks. He had found clumps of encrusted silver coins congealed in a solid mass from lying for centuries in salt water. It was treasure.

Luis grabbed Enrique's arm to get his attention and pointed to the black rock in his hand. Enrique dropped the debris he was carrying and took the rock from his father. He rolled it over in his hands looking at it from all sides. There was no doubt it was treasure. He could see the unmistakable circular shapes of coins in the black mass. He turned to his father with eyes wide in excitement and saw Luis picking up other black rocks. Enrique stuffed the softball-sized rock in his wet suit and helped his father gather more.

They made a pile of the black rocks and went to the surface, the air in their tanks just about expired.

"What took ya so long? Ya got it all cleaned up?" Chopper yelled from the air conditioned cab of the excavator.

Floating at the surface Luis spit out his mouthpiece, shoved his mask to his forehead and motioned for the barge to lift the platform of debris.

The father and son hid the excitement of their find from Chopper, the owner of the salvage company. They knew he would claim they were working for him and anything they found was his. They planned to come back later and recover the collection of encrusted coins that had been lying there since 1931 when the Russel twins boat, *Day Dreamer* sunk.

Chapter 6

Roberto Fuentes parked his pickup truck outside his brother's house, finding Luis in the cluttered garage. Roberto was at his brother's to borrow some money.

Luis excitedly told his brother about what he and Enrique discovered. Hoping to be a part of the treasure, Roberto said; "I know a guy who know dis stuff. I ask him ow much money it is, maybe?"

"Si, Roberto. Find out. There is enough for all of us."

Luis picked a clump of coins from one of the plastic buckets and with a screwdriver pried off a clump of three coins. "Take this to your man. Find how much," Luis told his brother.

Roberto didn't have any contacts in the rare coin world other than seeing signs in jewelry store windows advertising they sell shipwreck coins, mostly coins from the wreck of the *Atocha*. He pulled off U.S.1 at the first store he came to, Island Gems Jewelry.

"You know bout dis?" Roberto asked the man behind a glass case displaying silver coins, most hanging on a gold chain; known locally as a "Key West dog tag."

"Let me take a look," the man said reaching for the black clump. The man turned the coins over a few times in his palm, looked at it through a magnifying glass and said, "I'm not sure these are actual Spanish Reals." He placed it on a scale. Accounting for the centuries of corrosion and sea growth they were about the weight of three Spanish 8 Real coins and the diameter of the top coin measured just over an inch and a half, again the approximate size of an 8 Real.

"Where did you get these?" the jeweler asked.

"My brother find it," Roberto explained that his brother gave him the coins to find out if they were valuable and to find a buyer for them.

"Where?" the man asked.

"Don' know," Roberto replied. A fact Luis had not shared it with his brother.

"Well, let me show you something," the man said as he removed a coin from the display case and placed it next to Roberto's group of coins on a purple rectangle of velvet.

"Do you see the difference?"

Roberto looked down on the velvet where his black crusty coin was lying next to a shiny silver coin. "My is negro."

"Yes, it's black, but on mine you can clearly make out the design; see the shield and the pillars. On yours you can't see any design. That's why I think your coins are fake. It's probably toy pirate treasure coins you can buy in the shops. Maybe someone threw them in the ocean. I've seen parents toss them in the water for their kids to find."

Roberto didn't say anything; his dreams were being shattered.

"Look, I can give you $10.00 for the three of them. They're all black and look old, it's something the tourists will like. I'll be lucky to sell them for $12.00."

28

The disappointment was visible on Roberto's face. He had been dreaming of being rich and now he found out the treasure was just junk.

"No, no sell," Roberto said.

"Okay," the shop keeper said thinking, "I can go to $15.00 but I'm probably going to lose money."

"No, no sell." Roberto took the black clump of coins and turned to leave.

"Hey, hold on," the man yelled after Roberto. "Do you have any more of the coins? Maybe we can make a deal if you have more. Wait a second, let's talk."

The salesman watched Roberto walk to his truck and wrote a note; "Light green older Chevy pickup, faded red driver side door." Then grabbed his phone and punched in a number.

Roberto sat in his pickup in the parking lot staring out the windshield. He was upset that the coins his brother and nephew found might be worthless. Which meant his share for helping find a buyer for the coins was worthless too. He had dreams of being wealthy, driving a new truck, buying a big house on the ocean, but not now. He pulled out of the parking lot onto U.S.1 and was driving south when he saw another jewelry store advertising they sold treasure coins.

The woman behind the counter smiled and asked, "Can I help you?"

Roberto dug the mass of coins out from deep in his right jean pocket and asked, "You know this?"

The woman took the coins and looked at them, turning them over in her palm. She held it under a light and tried to scrape off some of the barnacles and other sea growth with a recently manicured fingernail. After another look at all sides of the black clump she walked down the display case, reached under the cash register and returned to Roberto. She handed him the coins back saying, "I don't know if it's valuable or a fake. We get a lot of guys trying to pass fake coins in here." She handed Roberto a business card and said, "Contact this guy. Whenever we have a question about the authenticity of a treasure coin we send it to him. He does our appraisal work and he will know if it is real and the value of it."

Sitting in the parking lot Roberto wasn't quite so disheartened. He thought, "Maybe they real and the other guy try steal 'em." He fished his phone out of his pocket and felt his right pocket for the second time to make sure the coins were still there then called Luis.

"Shit Luis where you are?" he said when Luis didn't answer. He looked at the business card the woman gave him. It read; *Undersea Archaeology of Miami,* Tim Main, Numismatic, Assayer, Marine Archaeologist. Roberto dialed the number.

"Hello, this is Tim Main, Marine Archaeologist with Undersea Archaeology of Miami. I can't come to the phone right now but please leave your name, phone number and a detailed message and I will get back to you as soon as I can."

Roberto answered, "I Roberto Fuentes, have black coins from water, I wan know ow much money it is." Then he left his phone number.

Chapter 7

"Luis, this is Roberto. I found guy who know treasure. He wan ta look at black coins." Roberto listened then said, "No, he smart, he look at coins for work. He wan ta see the black silver but he be in Miami. I gotta take it up to him in Miami. Luis I ain't got no gas. Ya got some money for me? Jus twenty for gas and fer sandwich, huh Luis? Ya got any?"

~ ~ ~

Roberto shook hands with Tim Main and handed him the black encrusted mass. "This it."

Tim, the numismatic for Undersea Archaeology of Miami took the black crusty coins from Roberto. "Please sit," he said motioning to a chair opposite his desk. Tim pushed his glasses up on his forehead and filpped on an illuminated magnifying glass to look closely at the clump of coins.

"It's hard to see any detail. The encrustations and oxidation needs to be removed before I can identify them."

Roberto, sitting on the edge of his seat, asked, "Is real?"

Turning the mass over several times under the magnifying glass, Main answered, "It's hard to tell in its present state, but I think so." He reached for a scale next to his desk and weighed the coins. "They're probably 8 Real, the weight is about right, but I won't be able to say for sure until it's cleaned up."

"How you clean?" Roberto asked.

The numismatic said, "There are a number of methods to clean a coin; the galvanic reduction method with an isopropyl alcohol and salt soak or electrolysis. With this I think we will use an electrolysis bath, and immerse the artifact in a 5 to 10% solution of caustic sodium hydroxide and water then pass an electrical charge through the artifact."

Roberto shook his head agreeing with the expert, although with a confused look on his face.

Tim could see he was losing Roberto by being too technical so he simply said, "We use various chemicals to remove all of this black and marine growth. It should only be done by a trained conservation professional or the coins can be damaged and their value severely diminished. One very important point is if you have any more of these coins you should keep them in salt water until they are cleaned. Exposure to air results in a highly accelerated rate of decomposition. So if you find any more keep them in a container of ocean water."

"Gold coins on the other hand do not corrode in salt water," Tim said venturing off topic, "and will typically have an encrustation that is greenish in color. Once the encrustation is removed gold coins are pretty much in the same condition as they were when they went down with the ship."

Roberto reluctantly agreed to leave the coins with the archaeologist so they could be cleaned and evaluated. Tim took photographs of all sides of the coins and filled out a detailed receipt for the mass of coins, which both men signed. "I should have the results in a few days and I'll get back to you."

As Roberto drove back down US1 towards the Keys he was thinking how happy he was with himself. His brother gave him a job and he didn't screw it up. He found an expert who was going to clean the coins and tell them how much they were worth. Roberto was smiling; he did good. He was going to be rich.

Rather than take US 1 from the Florida mainland into the Keys, Roberto decided to take the Card Sound Road. It was less traveled and Roberto could drink the six-pack he bought for lunch while he drove. Just past Alabama Jack's, Roberto drove over the toll bridge and popped the top on another beer. Before throwing the empty can out the window he checked the rear view mirror and noticed a car coming on fast. The car slowed as it got close to Roberto's pick-up and drove just a few feet behind.

Roberto slowed down for the car to pass. "Probably rich bastard from Ocean Reef," he said under his breath. "I be rich soon too. Maybe I move to Ocean Reef." The vehicle drifted towards the left lane to pass but its front bumper barely hit Roberto's rear bumper. Both vehicles slowed and pulled off on the gravel shoulder.

Roberto walked to the rear of his truck checking for damage as the driver of the black car got out apologizing. Not noticing any new damage on his already beat up truck Roberto said, "No worry." He turned to get back in his truck to the open beer he left sitting in the drink holder.

"Hey wait," the man called.

Roberto turned around to see the man holding a handgun pointed at his chest.

"Come with us. We want to talk with you," he said motioning towards his black Ford Explorer with dark tinted windows where another man stood holding a pistol.

Chapter 8

"Papa, you haven't told anyone about the coins, have you?" Enrique asked his father. "We said we would keep this a secret until we sold the silver."

"No. Jus you mama and Uncle Roberto."

"Papa, Papa, Papa, we said we weren't going to tell anyone. Remember, when we came back to the garage after picking up the silver, we promised not to tell anyone. Remember?"

"Si."

"Why did you tell your brother?"

"He know guy who know coins. Roberto help us. He take coin to a guy who knows about monedas de plata." Luis nervously resorted to mixing English and Spanish; referring to the silver coins as monedas de plata.

"Papa, we said we wouldn't tell anyone! Holy Mother of Jesus, Uncle Roberto can't keep his mouth shut and he took some coins to show someone. Now who else knows? We gotta hide the shit, before someone comes looking. Your brother is a screw up. He'll screw this up, you just watch and see."

"Enrique, I sorry, I mess up. I try to help, I din think right. Roberto won't tell, I told him he could have some of the plata if he find someone to buy it."

"Papa, it's too late to apologize, now we've got to get ahold of Uncle Roberto. Call him right now, and let me talk to him."

Luis pulled his cell phone out of his pocket flipped it open and said to his son, "I sorry, I mess up. I jus try help."

After four rings, Roberto's phone went to voice mail. "Roberto, this Luis, don tell no one bout..."

Enrique quickly grabbed his father's cell and flipped it closed before he could leave a message about a treasure in Spanish silver for anyone to hear.

"Papa, just let me handle everything. Don't tell anyone. I mean no one at all. "

"Ya wan me keep callin Roberto?"

"No!" Enrique yelled at his father, then felt bad for doing so. "I'm sorry. I'm sorry I yelled. No, I'll call Uncle Roberto. Don't talk to no one. No one! And tell Mama to keep quiet about the silver too."

Two and a half hours later on the eighth call Enrique made to his Uncle Roberto the phone was answered; "Hola."

Enrique quickly hung up ... it wasn't his uncle answering his uncle's phone.

Chapter 9

They parked their rental car off county road 905 on a secluded two track that was once State Road 4A. "Are you sure this is where it is?" Pam asked her husband Dave.

"Yeah, according to what I read on the internet and saw on the Google Earth image, the missile base is just north of here through the woods. It's going to be cool. We're going to be exploring a relic of the cold war," Dave said excitedly as he checked the contents of his back pack.

Pam looked around at the dense woods seeing a foot path leading off from the old road. "Is it legal for us to be here?" she asked Dave. "Or are army men going to come out of the woods with guns and arrest us?"

"Yeah, sort of legal. No, there is not a military presence here. This Nike Missile Control site has been abandoned since 1979."

Pam hefted her pack onto her back and asked, "Why is there a missile site in the Florida Keys in the first place? I mean, there wasn't a war or anything here, was there?"

"Honey, this was built in 1965 during the Cold War when Russia was building missile bases in Cuba. The United States built these bases as a defense against the Russian forces if it became necessary." Dave was a military history buff and considered his wife to be historically challenged. "The military also built missile installations on the beaches in Key West during that time."

Dave continued to tell Pam about the history of the missile site as they walked the path through the woods. "The missiles would have been fired down the road a couple of miles at the missile launch site. Where we are heading is the control site, designated HM-40. This is where they used sophisticated radar to watch for incoming missiles and track the missiles we launched. There were five radars, the target ranging radar, the target tracking radar, the missile tracking radar, the low power acquisition radar and the biggest was the high powered acquisition radar. They had both a low and high power acquisition radars in case the enemy tried to electronically jam the signal," Dave said as they walked showing off his knowledge. "The radars were mounted high off the ground on concrete pedestals and you can actually still see one of the pedestals from the highway.

Pam followed her husband through the overgrown trail, occasionally saying "Yes," or "Uh huh" so he would think she was paying attention, but in her mind she was on a sugar sand beach being served an umbrella drink by a handsome young, muscle bound mocha skin Caribbean man with dreadlocks hanging off his shoulders.

Dave continued reciting all he knew about the Nike Missile Control site HM-40. "The missile site was decommissioned in 1979 and the U.S. Fish and Wildlife Service owns it now. It's part of the Crocodile Lake National Wildlife Refuge."

Pam, still mentally sitting on a Caribbean beach said, "Uh huh. No. What? What about crocodiles? There are crocodiles here? You brought me in a jungle with crocodiles? Dave! I want to go back to the car right now!"

Dave trying to calm his wife's fear of the reptilian creatures said, "Don't worry, they won't hurt you. There are far worse things in the wildlife preserve."

Pam swiveling her head side to side looking for crocodiles asked, "What can be worse than a crocodile waiting to eat us?"

"Well, pythons have been found around here."

"Oh yeah, sure," Pam said scanning the sides of the path for anything moving.

Dave decided this was a teachable moment and began to tell Pam all he knew about the pythons in South Florida. "No Honey, I'm not kidding, people get a Burmese Python or other exotic snake as a pet and when they get bored with it or the snake gets too big to handle they tend to release them in the Everglades. And there was a snake farm in southern Florida that raised all types of snakes for the pet industry that was destroyed in a hurricane and all the snakes got loose and over the years they propagated and thrived. Now there are estimated to be 300,000 pythons in the Everglades and South Florida. In fact, the largest snake found in the Florida Keys was discovered near the Nike Missile site; a 16-footer."

"Dave! I'm going back to the car!" Pam yelled at her husband. "I mean it! I'm going back with or without you. I can't believe you brought me out here in the jungle with crocodiles and snakes all around. I am so pissed at you!"

"Okay, okay, we can go back," Dave said reluctantly knowing there was no way he was going to get Pam to go to the missile site with him. Realizing his desire to show off his knowledge of Key's wildlife backfired on him.

They turned back along the trail, Pam making Dave walk in front of her to scare away any creatures ready to eat them or wrap their slimy body around them and squeeze them until their eyes popped out.

"Are you mad at me for not telling you about the snakes and crocs?" Dave asked, slowing down for her answer.

She pushed him in the back and said, "Keep moving! Yes, I'm pissed at you. Don't expect any sex for a while either!"

"Shit!" Dave said, as he suddenly stopped. Pam, looking to the side, ran into his back. "Pam don't look to the left, just run."

In the safety of the car, with the windows up and the doors locked, Pam frantically asked, "What was it? Was it a snake? Was it a crocodile? God, I am so pissed at you! What was it, answer me damn it!"

Dave didn't answer, he was dialing 911 on his cell phone.

Chapter 10

"It's over here," the deputy said leading the detective through the thick woods off county road 905. "The couple who discovered the victim are over there in that red Mustang. The woman is still shaking and she is not happy with her husband. They have been fighting since we got here."

After a short walk through the thick overgrowth, the deputies came to a woman encased in a white Tyvek suit kneeling over the body. She nodded acknowledgement of the detective. "What ya got, Terry?" he asked looking down at the man lying in the brush.

The crime scene investigator said, "Well, the only thing I can tell you for sure is he was killed somewhere else and dumped here."

"How long has he been dead?"

"Based on a field estimation I would say about three days. How long he has been here, I don't know. The cause of death was probably the gunshot to the back of his head."

The detective looked at her with a questioning look and asked, "Probably? Isn't a gunshot to the head enough?"

"Yeah, but until I get him back to the lab I can't be sure if it was a bullet to the brain or the beating the man took is what actually killed him. He was tortured before death," she said picking up the victims left arm to display recent cigarette burns and knife slashes. She put it down and lifted his right hand to show the detective how the man's fingers were distorted from someone twisting them out of joint and breaking them. "Some mean son of a bitch really didn't like this guy. Oh, and his penis was cut off too."

The detective looked at the blood stain at the crotch of the man's jeans. "Yeah, I see that. Find it?"

"Yeah, it's stuffed in his shirt pocket." She pointed to the breast pocket in the man's tee shirt. The detective noticed the piece of flesh peeking over the top of the pocket.

The detective turned to the deputy and asked, "Any ID?"

"No. Nothing on him. We'll get prints later."

"So, someone tortured him, and killed him and left him near a trail used by the military history nuts. They wanted him found. They are sending a message to someone. A message that says, 'This could happen to you.'"

The detective looked down at the man with a face swollen from the beating he endured and peppered with welts and open sores where the bugs and rats chewed on him and asked, "Who did you piss off so much that they beat the shit out of you? What did you know that someone else wanted to know? What was it that was so important to you that you took a vicious beating and didn't tell, or did you?"

Chapter 11

Tim Main was both pleased yet perplexed when he saw the Fuentes coins after the techs ran them through the electrolysis bath. The coins shined brilliantly under the LED light of the magnifying glass. Tim turned them over several times in a cotton-gloved hand. They were all the shield type coin, which were minted in the New World. The design was clearly visible and distinctive. One side had the characteristic shield with multiple designs representing the lands of the Spanish territory. The other side displayed a cross with lions and castles.

He knew historically the coin was struck at the Mexico, Santo Domingo, Lima, La Plata, Potosi, Panama, Cartagena, and Bogotá mints during the time period of 1572 to 1734. The coins from the era included the year it was minted and a distinctive mark to identify the city where it was minted. But the Fuentes coins did not show any date or mint marks which indicated they were very old, probably from a shipwreck prior to 1607, the year they began putting a year on the coins. Coins from this era were very rare and when discovered they were hardly ever in such good condition. Tim wondered if Mr. Fuentes had any more of the coins and where they were discovered. The coins could be very valuable and a historically important discovery.

Tim poured over his research looking for a known Spanish Treasure ship that would have run aground on the reef off the Florida Keys carrying such an old treasure in silver. He dated the coin prior to 1607 but from his research he could not find a treasure ship that went down during that time period.

After several calls went unanswered, Tim decided to drive down to the Keys to the address Roberto provided on the receipt. He needed to return the coins and he wanted to get more information from a historical perspective like precisely where the coins were found. Tim concluded the coins must be from a previously undiscovered and undocumented shipwreck and from an archaeological perspective that would be significant.

Tim drove down the Florida Turnpike to Florida City where he exited onto US1. From there he drove along the 18-mile stretch, a section of US1 connecting the mainland of the Florida peninsula and the island of Key Largo. He always enjoyed the trip to the Keys, passing through the southern edge of the Everglades, on the recently reconstructed road with its turquoise concrete lane dividers and the view of boats on the intercostal waterway from the top of the Jewfish Creek Bridge.

Whenever Tim approached a passing lane the cars behind him would fly by. But he wasn't in a hurry and drove the speed limit. Just about all the cars on the stretch were doing well over the limit except he and the black SUV that had been behind him since he left the mainland. As he slowed and entered Key Largo Tim could feel the stress of working and driving in Miami fade away.

Tim pulled off the highway at a gas station for an iced tea and a bathroom break. When he returned to his car he noticed the black SUV or one like it, with dark tinted windows parked in the lot. He climbed into his car and a man approached and said. "Hey mister, hold on; I want to ask you something."

Tim ignored him, figuring the man was begging money. He started his car, locked the doors and the air conditioner and radio drowned out the man. The beggar tapped on Tim's driver side window and said, "Hey, just a minute man, I wanna talk to you."

Tim continued to ignore the man. The guy tapped on the window again and lifted his tee shirt revealing a gun in his pant waist and demanded, "Open up!"

Tim slammed the transmission into drive and mashed down on the accelerator. The car sped forward with a screeching of the tires. At the highway Tim saw a small opening in the south bound traffic and took it. The driver of the car he cut off slammed on his brakes and flashed him the finger. In his rear view mirror, Tim saw the man with the gun jump in the passenger side of a black Ford Explorer.

Tim raced down US1 passing cars on the left and right, hoping if he broke the speed limit a cop would pull him over. As he removed his cell phone from his left front pant pocket he realized he hadn't fastened his seat belt. In the excitement he hadn't noticed the beeping of the seat belt alarm but wasn't going to take the time now. Holding the steering wheel with one hand, passing a semi-truck and trying to dial 911 he fumbled the phone dropping it on the floor. Driving 72 miles per hour in a 45 zone he reached down between his legs to retrieve the phone.

The car ahead of him slowed to turn left, Tim swerved into the right lane, the right wheels of his car left the roadway. Tim's car traveled across the gravel of the shoulder, over the grass at the side of the road and smashed head-on into a concrete power pole.

Chapter 12

Mark and Sherry Daniels loved their condominium in the Florida Keys. Located between Key Largo and Islamorada in Tavernier, the location suited them well. It was close enough to Key West to drive down there for a day but far enough away from the crowds that packed the southernmost island.

At the condo they made friends from all over the country who also wintered in the Keys. They relaxed on the beach and gathered for sunset. Sherry, with time on her hands, bought a sketchpad and pastel pencils, picking up where she left off nearly 27 years ago when their daughter Mandy was born.

Mark reclined on a lounge chair with the spiral bound notebook propped up on his knees. It contained notes and chapters of the "Great American Novel" he was writing. Its current working title was *Death on the Water,* although it was subject to change; it had already been titled; The Lethal Lake, Beach Party Murders, and Swim, Float and Die.

The novel was his way to keep his mind active after retiring from the Detroit Free Press as a crime scene reporter where he specialized in murder. The novel he was working on was about a sadistic killer loose at the Lake of the Ozarks in Missouri, killing residents and visitors enjoying the popular recreational destination.

"Are you working on the novel?" Sherry asked.

Mark was staring out at the water of Florida Bay lost in thought. "Huh? Are you talking to me?" he said drifting back to reality.

"Oh, never mind," Sherry said. "Are you going back to the condo before long?" she asked.

"Yeah," Mark said as he took a sip of his iced tea. "I'm not getting anywhere with the book; the juices just aren't flowing today. I might go up and get something to read. What do you want?"

"Could you get me a bottle of water, please? A nice cold one," Sherry said.

Mark gathered his notebook and file folder containing printed copies of research; pages of facts and charts of the Lake of the Ozarks, "Sure, I've got to pee anyway."

Sherry layed back on her lounge chair, adjusted her visor to block the sun from her eyes and said, "I'll be here."

Mark stood, slipped on his flip flops, and with notebook and file in hand looked at his wife and thought, She'll be asleep before I get back.

Mark left the beach and walked to the condo parking lot on his way to the staircase up to the second floor units. As he walked, he was thinking of past murders he covered as a reporter that he might use in the book. He was about to climb the stairs when he heard a loud crash and the blaring of a car horn.

Mark ran towards US1, finding a car had run off the road and smashed head-on into a concrete power pole. Mark, the first to arrive, ran towards the driver's side door and attempted to open it and get the driver out but the damage had jammed the door, it wouldn't open.

Mark quickly ran around the car to the passenger side door.

Mark opened the door and looked in at the driver. The man's head was against the steering wheel turned towards Mark, his arms limp at his sides and blood flowed from a gash on the man's forehead covering his face. Pink foamy spittle dripped from the corner of his mouth and his eyes stared blankly.

He threw his notebook and file on the seat and reached for the driver. He carefully lifted the man's head off the steering wheel and leaned him back in the seat. Mark's hand was bloody and wiped his fingers as best he could on the back of the seat.

Mark looked for signs of life but there wasn't any discernible movement of his chest and no sign of inhaling or exhaling from his nose or mouth. Mark reached to the man's wrist to feel for a pulse, then to his neck. He didn't feel anything.

Mark was about to pull the man out of the car for cardio pulmonary compressions when the fire rescue trucks arrived. Mark backed out the passenger door and looked back in at the man, Mark was pretty sure he was dead. As he moved away from the crumpled car, Mark noticed his notebook lying on the passenger's seat. He reached in and grabbed the notebook and file, just before the paramedic in an orange jump suit and purple rubber gloves climbed in.

No one noticed a small non-descript brown envelope that had fallen between the passenger seat and the center console. The envelope contained the three silver coins Tim was returning to Roberto. The envelope would later be discovered by an unscrupulous insurance adjuster and not returned.

A crowd had gathered. Several cars had stopped and a sheriff's deputy was waving the slow moving traffic past the accident, the drivers craning their necks, gawking in fascination trying to get a glimpse of the victim. The traffic included a black Ford Explorer with tinted windows.

Mark was talking to a deputy when Sherry and a group from the beach arrived, curious what all the sirens were about. The Deputy asked him to step to his car so he could type Mark's information into his onboard computer. Mark handed his notebook to Sherry, telling her he would be right back.

~ ~ ~

The accident was the talk of the Anchor Condominiums Sunset Celebration that evening. In response to the morbid curiosity of the group, Mark repeated what he knew, several times to different people who asked. He was asked several times: Was the guy dead? Was he alive when Mark got there? What were the man's last words before he died? Why did he run off the road into a power pole? Was he drunk? Was he on drugs? Was he alone? Was it a suicide? Was he a local or a tourist? Mark answered, "I don't know," to most questions. Mark really didn't know the answers, except that he was pretty sure the man was dead when he got to the car.

Chapter 13

The morning after the car crashed into the power pole Mark was up early as usual, sitting on the balcony overlooking the calm blue water of Florida Bay and the gently swaying palm trees. He had a coffee on the table next to him and the computer on his lap. Mark first checked flkeysnews.com looking for information about the accident. He found out the man killed was Tim Main from Fort Lauderdale. He was survived by Lynn, his wife, and two children.

That was all that Mark knew of the man, a man who came into his life so dramatically, imprinting a horrific and tragic memory in Mark's mind. Throughout his career as a crime reporter, Mark had been to many crime scenes and seen many dead bodies, but this time he was the first person at the scene of a death and was required to surveil the situation and take action.

Mark wondered if he should have touched the body at all, but removing the man's head from the steering wheel seemed like the right thing to do. Maybe subconsciously he did it to stop the horn from blaring, maybe he did it to check if the man had a pulse, he didn't really know why he eased the man's bloody head off the steering wheel and back against the head rest. But Mark was pretty sure the man wasn't breathing. He was ready to pull the man from the car to administer chest compressions but the paramedic showed up before he could do anything. The paramedic later told him that the man's chest was so severely crushed from impacting the steering wheel at a high rate of speed without wearing a seatbelt that any attempt to resuscitate would only have resulted in further damage.

Sherry walked out to the balcony and looked at the table for her creamer and coffee. With hands on her hips she asked in mock disgust, "Did you forget about me?"

It was their morning routine; Mark rose early and made coffee and when he heard his wife stirring two hours later, he would make her a cup of her favorite morning concoction; one-part coffee to three parts French vanilla creamer.

"Oh sorry hon, I was looking for information about the accident. I'll go get your morning elixir."

Sherry sat down and opened the iPad to see what was new on Facebook and Mark went to the kitchen to make Sherry's creamer and coffee. He didn't mind; he needed a break from the laptop and the tragic death of Mr. Tim Main.

Their plans for the day were pretty much like every other day, breakfast on the balcony, sitting on the beach reading, writing or napping, dinner on the balcony or fresh fish at one of the waterfront restaurants they had discovered. Then they would meet with the other residents of the condo to socialize and celebrate the setting of the sun.

After lunch of tuna salad and fruit, which was Sherry's idea of a healthy meal, but Mark figured she was trying to starve him to death, Sherry went to the beach. She found two lounge chairs next to one another that were partially shaded by palm trees. She spread out her towel and reclined.

Before he left the condo, Mark snuck a couple chocolate chip cookies to supplement his lunch then grabbed his writing materials from the desk. Armed with his notebook, the file folder of research, a pencil, an iced tea and a towel over his shoulder, Mark was ready for a day at the beach.

Sherry was busy talking to Diane, Karen and Sue about the books they each were reading when Mark kicked off his sandals, laid back on the chair and opened up his notebook. He reviewed what he had written yesterday about a murderer preying on the people of Lake of the Ozarks and jotted some notes in the margins. He was at the point where he needed his antagonist to murder the high school football coach and was trying to come up with a unique way to do away with him. Mark had already left the dead body of a tourist sitting in an anchored row boat, propped up with a fishing pole duct taped in his hands. Boaters went back and forth by the dead guy, some waving, some yelling at the fisherman because he was anchored in a busy part of the lake, just across from the Alhonna Resort.

Mark wondered if he looked at a nautical chart of the lake maybe he would get inspiration. He moved his notebook aside to check the pages of research he kept in the manila file folder. There were two files. Mark looked again, he only had one file of research but now there were two.

He opened the cover of the second file and looked at the first page. He didn't recognize it as anything of his. It was a report about Spanish ships that sank off the Florida Keys. He looked at the list; *Herrera, Nuestra Señora del Populo, El Gallo Indiano, El Infante, El Rubi, San Felipe, also known as El Lerri* or *El Terri, Nuestra Señora de Atocha, San Francisco, Santa Margarita and Tres Puentes.* The only ship that was familiar to Mark was the *Atocha.* It was the ship Mel Fisher discovered off Key West with millions of dollars in silver, gold, and jewels.

Mark flipped through the pages finding photocopies of what looked like old Spanish coins with a page or two narrative describing each. He found copies of marine charts showing the location of wrecks along the reef off the Keys. There were other charts that showed locations along the coast where treasure had been discovered.

"Where the hell did this come from?" Mark said, turning the pages over and reviewing them. "This isn't anything of mine. It doesn't make sense. It was in my pile of stuff but it's not mine?" Mark suddenly became aware that he was sitting on the beach talking out loud to himself. He quickly looked around, but no one seemed to notice.

There has to be forty, fifty pages of information about Spanish galleons that sank or disappeared off the coast of the Florida Keys, Mark thought. There was a page or two about each ship; type of ship, cargo carried, year of wreck, disposition of the ship, crew and cargo. Mark flipped the folder closed looking at the cover. It was just a common Manila folder, nothing written on it not even on the index tab. Mark flipped the folder over, all he saw was a brownish stain, like someone with chocolate on their fingers smeared it on the folder. Nothing that could help him identify where the folder came from or whose it was. "Where the hell did this come from?" Mark mumbled.

"Are you talking to yourself?" Sherry asked as she returned and lowered herself onto the lounge.

"No. Well yes, I guess," Mark stammered, lost in his state of confusion. "This folder was in my pile of stuff on the desk but it's not mine. Do you know where it came from?"

Sherry glanced at the folder Mark was holding up, "Nope. Never saw it. You know I don't touch your writing stuff."

"I know, but this isn't mine, I never saw it before and yet here it is with my file of research. Where did it come from?" Mark asked as he thumbed through the pages. "Like here is a page with a picture of a silver coin enlarged and along the margins someone wrote notes in blue ink."

"What does it say?" Sherry asked.

Mark balanced the folder and stack of pages against his thighs as he sat in the lounge chair. He took out the coin page and turned it sideways to read one of the comments. "Struck at the Mexico, Santo Domingo, Lima, La Plata, Potosi, Panama, Cartagena, and Bogota mints."

Mark turned the page in the other direction and read, "1572 to 1734."

Sherry settled back with her iPad and said, "Well, you let me know if you find some of those pirate treasure coins. Real ones, not those paper ones."

Mark smiled at his wife and said, "You mean Re-al coins."

Sherry looked at her husband quizzically.

Mark explained a Spanish coin was called a Real.

Mark returned the page to its location in the stack of paper. He tapped the file on its end to straighten the papers, laid the file on his stomach, leaned back and closed his eyes. He wasn't going to fall asleep as he was known to do as he laid on the beach, rather his mind was reviewing the events that just occurred; finding a file on his desk that wasn't his, the file consisting of information about Spanish galleons, silver coins, shipwrecks, and treasure. And wondering where it came from and what it all meant.

Mark thought Sherry was asleep and was surprised when she said. "Mark; you were at the Islamorada library last week. Maybe you picked up someone else's file there."

Mark thought about it and said," You know you are probably right. I might have accidently picked up some research someone else was doing. Next time we are that way I'll stop in and ask at the desk if anyone reported missing a file folder of information about Spanish coins."

Thinking about the coins got the best of Mark and he told Sherry, "I'm going up to the room. I've got some things I want to look up on the internet."

Chapter 14

While Sherry went out to lunch with some other ladies from the condo, Mark settled down in a lounge chair on the beach. He had an iced tea on the table next to him, a towel bunched up behind his lower back, his notebook leaned against his propped up knees and a pencil in hand. He was going to take advantage of the time to write without Sherry interrupting him. He re-read where he left off on his novel about a murderer loose at the Lake of the Ozarks, turned his mind loose and started writing.

"I am going to take the kayak out for a while," *Bonnie Kyriss told her husband, Darrell.*

"Okay, be careful. I would go with you but I have to have this proposal finished by 4:00 today. I'll be glued to the computer till then."

"I will, I'm just going to hug the shore and look for creatures in the shallows. And you were the one who wanted to come to the lake to get away for a few days."

Bonnie walked down to the boathouse at the water's edge, her blond ponytail sticking out the back of her baseball cap bounced with each step. She looked at their 29-foot custom painted Hustler high performance boat powered by two 540 horsepower Mercury Racing engines sitting high on a lift. It was something Darrell had to have when they bought their 3,000 square foot "cottage" on the lake. Bonnie knew her husband and knew he bought it to impress. Darrell would occasionally lower the boat into the water and start it up. He would rev the engines incessantly and pretend he was tinkering with the motors or the several-thousand-dollar navigation system. But Darrell rarely took the boat away from the dock.

Bonnie preferred the kayak. It was quiet, peaceful, and most importantly, Darrell wasn't with her constantly talking on his cell phone. She could just paddle and silently glide over the water and look for fish or other wildlife near the shore. At times she stopped to do her environmental duty of picking up beer cans and empty bait containers from the bottom.

Bonnie opened the door to the boathouse and stepped in. With her eyes accustomed to the bright sun she was blind in the dark confines of the building. Rather than wait for her eyes to adjust she felt her way across the small room to the kayak paddles leaning against the rear wall. In total darkness Bonnie was startled when she bumped face first into something cool and clammy hanging from the rafters. "Damn it Darrell," she thought, "Why can't you put the life jackets in the dock storage box instead of throwing them over the rafters. It scared the hell out of me."

As Bonnie's eyes adjusted to the dim light, she slowly realized it wasn't a damp life jacket carelessly thrown over the boathouse rafters that she walked into, it was the cold lifeless body of Lenny Puff, the high school football coach. His head hung awkwardly from the noose around his neck, his dead glassy eyes stared at the floor.

Mark was startled and jumped when Sherry kissed him on the head and said, "Hi sweetie, I'm back." He was so engrossed with the dead body of the coach found hanging in a dark and dank boathouse that he didn't realize she had returned from lunch with the girls.

She pulled a lounge chair next to Mark and began to tell him about the fish tacos she had for lunch at the Island Grill Restaurant and filled him in on all of the condo gossip she heard.

Mark closed his notebook and took a sip of his tea. He was done writing, Sherry was back.

"What are you doing?" she asked.

"Oh, I was just murdering someone."

"You know you find so many inventive ways to murder people that I'm getting a little concerned for my safety," she said leaning back in her chair.

"You need not worry my dear. You are much too pretty to shoot, stab, poison, hang, choke, incinerate, or chop up into small pieces."

Sherry leaned over, patted his arm and said, "Aww Mark you say the sweetest things."

It wasn't long and Sherry no longer said anything. She was sound asleep. Mark decided to take advantage of her mid-day nap and write some more about the death of the football coach but soon realized his creative spark was doused. He set the notebook aside and opened the folder about shipwrecks and treasure.

Mark was still perplexed about where the file folder had come from. He checked at the Islamorada library to see if anyone had reported losing a file folder but the librarian didn't know anything about it. He mentally backtracked his travels in the last week or so but couldn't figure out where he picked up the mysterious file folder.

Starting on the first page Mark began reading. Before long he opened his notebook to record pertinent information. At the top of the page he wrote, "Shipwrecks of 1733."

In outline form Mark jotted down notes for future reference:

- July 13, 1733 departed Havana on return trip to Spain.
- Fleet consisted of 4 gunships - protection.
- 16 merchant ships, 2 ships with supplies for St. Augustine.
- Day after leaving wind shifted -increased.
- Fearing a hurricane, Commander ordered the ships to return to Havana.
- Some ships made it to Havana.
- One made it on to Spain.
- Thirteen others sunk, grounded or swamped along 80 mile stretch of the Florida Keys.
- Rescue boats sailed to find survivors and salvage cargo.
- Ships that could not be refloated were burned to the waterline, making it easier for divers to recover cargo in the hold and to keep the vessel out of hands of pirates.
- Ironically, after recovery efforts it was discovered that more gold and silver was recovered than what was listed on the manifests, evidence the ships were carrying a large amount of unregistered cargo.

Mark read with fascination. The information in the mysterious file was a virtual encyclopedia of the 1733 Spanish fleet that had sunk along the Keys in a hurricane. The next several pages were details about each ship of the 1733 fleet. Mark took notes.

Sueco de Arizon

- Sunk off Conch Key.
- Smaller vessel, it was carried into shallow water, only nine feet.
- All that remains are mounds of river rock used as ballast.
- Location: 24° 46.62 'N 80° 53.372 W
- Cargo: Silver, porcelain, leather, hides, cochineal, indigo and tobacco.

Nuestra Senora dee las Angustias

- Off Long Key Channel
- Cargo; indigo, cochineal dyes, Mexican silver and Chinese porcelain.
- Location: 24° 47.455 N   80° 51.738 W

San Felipe, aka El Terri, El Lerri, and Therry

- Off Lower Matecumbe Key in 15 feet of water.
- Cargo: silver, cochineal, indigo, chocolate, molasses, citrus relish, tobacco
- Located: 24° 50.761 N   80° 42.850 W

Mark read through all thirteen wrecks of the fleet of 1733 and studied the map in the file showing the location where each galleon grounded or sank. The *Populo* was grounded to the north on Elliot Key near Biscayne Bay and the rest of the fleet that did not make it back to Havana were scattered along the keys.

Mark found a common denominator amongst the ships destroyed in the 1733 hurricane. They were all carrying silver from the mines of south and central America back to Spain. He thought, even if 90% of the treasure was recovered, that would still leave a lot of silver laying around to be discovered by future generations.

The next several pages of the mystery file contained photographs, drawings and narrative about gold and silver coins. Some of the coins were found washed up individually on the beaches near the shipwrecks of the fleet and some were discovered in congealed clumps.

Mark began reading the next section. It was a narrative written about what Mark deducted were three coins. The first few pages described in technical terms the condition of the coins and the process used to clean them. The next pages went into specific information about the type of silver coins carried on the fleet of 1733. At the end of the dissertation was a paragraph that stated the coins that were cleaned were not from the 1733 fleet. They were much older coins, without a mint date and considering their uncirculated condition, they must have been minted and lost prior to 1607. It was a high degree of probability that the coins were from a ship that had gone aground on the reef over a hundred years before the fleet of 1733. Since a search of maritime records did not reveal a vessel with a cargo of silver grounding on the reef during that time period, the author of the document declared the coins must be from a previously undiscovered ship, a ship that would be of huge interest to maritime historians.

Mark was very interested in what he was reading. He was thinking that it would make a good book. The information he was reading included pirates and sunken treasure. "I wonder where the 3 coins were found? I don't think it was mentioned," although looking at the stack of papers remaining to be read he realized he still had a lot to learn.

Chapter 15

"Welcome aboard, ladies and gentlemen. I'm Captain Greg and I'll be at the helm for today's voyage out on the waters of the Atlantic Ocean. The weather looks fantastic, a high of 78 degrees. For our Canadian friends aboard that's about 25 Celsius. Beats the heck out of back home, eh? It's a perfect day in the beautiful Florida Keys!"

"The life jackets, if for some strange reason we need them are located above your head in the ceiling of the cabin and *Mermaid Dreams* is equipped with a 25 passenger life raft which is mounted on the roof of the cabin that deploys automatically," Captain Greg carefully avoided the phrase, "In case *Mermaid Dreams* sinks."

"Gather around the railing and look down through the glass bottom of the boat. Through that glass you will see, ancient coral, giant sea rays, shipwrecks and maybe a man eating shark or two."

"Before we depart the dock, does anyone have any questions? No? Well get ready for a thrill of a lifetime as we go out into the ocean and see nature's splendor. And if you enjoy the trip show some kindness to the crew in the tip jar located near the helm. Remember, wind and waves can rock the boat, but only you can tip the crew!"

The twin diesel engines of *Mermaid Dreams* roared to life, black smoke bellowing from the exhaust, dock lines were cast off and the 45-foot vessel backed away from the dock. The course *Mermaid Dreams* would follow took the boat through the entrance of the Boot Key Harbor at Marathon and out into the open water. Captain Greg would first take the tourists over a coral shelf to show them the material that formed the islands thousands of years ago, then out to a pile of ballast stones that were all that remained of a Spanish galleon that ran aground on the reef centuries ago. The tour then traveled around the East Washerwoman lighthouse and back to the marina. It was the same tour twice a day.

The tourists ranging from 5 years old to 87 jostled with each other trying to get a good spot along the railing to take photos of the coral through the glass bottom. Captain Greg explained through the public address system of *Mermaid Dreams* that, "Coral is called the "rainforests of the sea", and are some of the most diverse ecosystems on Earth. Most coral reefs are built from polyps that cluster in groups. The coral secretes a hard carbonate exoskeleton which support and protect the coral polyps. The coral grow best in warm, shallow, clear, sunny and agitated waters. Over the years these coral build on one another and form a hard coral reef. The islands of the Florida Keys are examples of coral reefs."

"Next," Captain Greg announced, "we're heading to the site of the sunken ship."

The GPS beeped alerting the captain he was nearing the wreck site. Captain Greg pulled back on the throttles, slowing the boat as they approached the pile of ballast stones, all that remained of a ship that ran aground on the reef hundreds of years ago. *Mermaid Dreams* crept slowly along the sandy bottom trying not to churn up the sand and cloud the visibility.

The captain began his narration: "The shipwreck you are about to see was part of a Spanish treasure fleet that was carrying millions of dollars in gold, silver and jewels." Actually Captain Greg didn't know what ship the ballast stones came from and it was in such shallow water that any cargo the vessel carried probably would have been easily recovered.

The guests became excited as the stones came into view through the glass bottom of the boat. They lined the railing with their cameras and cell phones snapping photographs of the pile of stones and the fish that called it home. A school of trigger fish swam in unison near the stones, a lobster scurried back into the protection of its lair and sergeant-majors and grunts swam around seemingly unaware of the boat.

As *Mermaid Dreams* slowly drifted over the remains of the galleon, the captain hyped the experience by asking for a moment of silence out of respect for the crew of the galleon who lost their lives when the ship was broken apart in a ferocious hurricane. Of course he had no idea if anyone was killed when the ship grounded.

As the captain stood at the wheel, the respectful silence of the passengers turned to screams of terror. As *Mermaid Dreams* slowly drifted over the sandy bottom, a 22-foot open powerboat lying upright on the bottom came into view. Sitting at the helm of the boat was a man, starring off in the distance. His long gray hair flowed on the current, his face was pale white and fish nibbled at the gash in his neck.

~ ~ ~

Deputy Skinner parked next to the ambulance. There already was a Florida Fish and Wildlife Conservation pick-up truck on site. He walked to the "fish cop" and asked what he knew.

"Our boat is out there now and will be bringing the vic in a while. The guy looks like he was beaten to death before the boat was scuttled. They radioed in that there was a dock line around his waist tying him to the helm seat and his shoe laces were used to tie his hands to the wheel. I guess someone wanted to make it look good for the tourists on the glass bottom boat."

"Yeah," Deputy Skinner said, "they wanted him found or they would have dumped him in deep water. And since the boat was sunk next to the old pile of ballast stones that the glass bottom boat goes over a couple of times a day it's fairly obvious they wanted to make finding him a big deal. They are probably making a statement to someone."

"Yep, that was what I was thinking too," the Florida Fish and Wildlife officer said.

Deputy Skinner said, "I bet it's a drug thing, maybe this guy shorted a delivery or a cash payment and they wanted to send a message to their other associates that that kind of shit ain't tolerated. Any identification?"

"Nothing yet. The fish have been feasting on his face and the saltwater has the corpse all swollen and shit. Hell I doubt his own mother would recognize him."

Chapter 16

Mark got up, made a pot of coffee, and settled down on his chair on the balcony. With a hot cup of coffee at his side and the computer on his lap Mark opened the Detroit Free Press website and said to himself, "Let's see what has been happening up in "The D". Mark recognized fewer and fewer names in the newspaper bylines. It's to be expected he thought. He had retired from the Free Press five years earlier and new reporters had moved in, just like when he was the new young reporter and other guys retired.

A sip of his rapidly cooling coffee and he opened the Florida Keys news site. Not much caught his attention as he skimmed the headlines; a traffic accident on the seven-mile bridge, a domestic violence case on Cudjoe Key, and a letter to the editor about genetically modified mosquitos.

Being a retired reporter whose specialty was covering murders, even earning the nickname the *Correspondent of Corpses,* Mark was automatically drawn to the headline about a dead body found in the middle Keys of Florida. He clicked on the headline and the article appeared.

As Mark read he became more interested in the death. It was just the type of murder that piqued his curiosity; a dead body found tied to a boat in 13 feet of water. The article went on to say that the man's death was being investigated and more information would be released as it became available.

"I'll have to remember to check back and see what this is all about," Mark mumbled to himself as he heard Sherry moving around upstairs. He got up to mix Sherry her morning French vanilla and coffee blend.

They settled down on the balcony overlooking Florida Bay and sipped their morning brews, Sherry checking Facebook and Mark looking for interesting murders when Sherry broke the peaceful solitude. "We need to defriend that friend of yours from college." Sherry looked at the screen, "Dave somebody. I am sick of his political rants."

Mark looked up from the laptop and answered, "Go ahead." Then he went back to reading about a missing woman in Montana.

"Mark," Sherry interrupted her husband again, "don't forget it's laundry day. Make sure all of your dirty clothes are in the hamper."

"Okay," Mark said trying to finish the article about the Montana woman missing and feared dead in the national forest.

A few minutes later Sherry said, "Do you remember, Peggy Johnson? She and I taught together?"

Mark looked up from the computer a little irritated at being interrupted again, "Yeah, pretty woman with long reddish blond hair."

Sherry said, "Well, I should have guessed you would remember the pretty woman with long reddish blond hair."

Mark closed the laptop, realizing he wasn't going to get anything done with Sherry sitting next to him bugging him.

"What about Peggy Johnson?" he asked, a bit frustrated.

"Nothing. She and a girlfriend are wintering in Florida. She posted a few pictures of them on Clearwater beach, that's all. And no, you can't see the pictures."

The laundry was done, folded and put away before lunch. Now it was time to relax on the beach. Mark took his notebook and file of Lake of the Ozarks research and the mysterious folder about Spanish silver and sunken ships. As he lowered his body onto the cushioned chair and balled up his towel behind his back for lumbar support, he sipped his tall iced tea with a splash of rum and looked out over the waters of the bay. Sherry relaxed talking to their daughter on her cell.

Mark reached into the canvas bag Sherry hauled to the beach and took out the iPad. He checked to see if there was any more information about the body found tied to a boat off Boot Key Harbor.

Mark clicked on a headline and read that the body was that of 63-year-old Michael "Chopper" Wirsbinski, owner of Sunshine Marine Salvage on Fat Deer Key. The article went on to say the death was being investigated as a homicide. I'll have to keep checking to see what this is all about, Mark thought. I've never been known to be one to ignore a good homicide.

Another headline caught his attention, "Body discovered in North Key Largo." The article said little other than a body was discovered. Mark wondered if it was a homicide, a suicide or an accidental death. It was another article he would have to follow.

The next day Mark was eager to check for any new information on the guy they found dead in water off Marathon. The article hadn't changed but there were comments made by readers that Mark found interesting.

Bikini Deb said: "He was a great guy; he will be missed. RIP Chopper."

Jersey Terry wrote: "I heard he got rich finding pirate treasure."

P. Pieper added, "I bet he died protecting his stash of booty. I heard he discovered as much treasure as Mel Fisher, he just didn't tell the government so he wouldn't have to share it with them."

So he was involved with sunken treasure? Mark thought, now this is getting interesting. Maybe he found some treasure while he was salvaging stuff off the bottom. Maybe he came across some gold from the Spanish treasure fleet that ran up on the reef during the 1733 hurricane, or plunder from a pirate's ship. Too bad he is dead. He might have been able to help out with the information in the mystery file.

Mark was thinking, I wonder if Michael "Chopper" Wirsbinski was murdered for the treasure he found on the bottom." He jotted down notes in his notebook about Chopper Wirsbinski and the rumors of treasure.

Chapter 17

"What do you feel like doing today?" Sherry asked as she sipped her morning creamer and coffee.

Mark looked up from the always-present computer on his lap, stared out at the water and sky and said, "It looks pretty gray out there, I think The Weather Channel called for rain before noon. Maybe we should take a ride somewhere."

Sherry, always ready for a road trip said, "Fine with me, where would you like to go? Up to Key Largo or down to Islamorada? There is a sandal store I really like in either direction."

"I was thinking of taking a ride down to Marathon."

"Marathon?" Sherry said surprised Mark wanted to drive almost fifty miles down the Keys in the congested US1 traffic. "Sure, let's go. I could stand getting out of the condo for a day. And there is a sandal shop there too. What about the rain?"

"According to the radar it's going to rain here but not down there. When will you be ready?" Mark asked shutting down the computer and closing his notebook.

Sherry stood, finished her coffee and said, "Give me 10 or 15 minutes and I'll be clean and beautiful."

Mark opened up the computer knowing that he had at least 45 minutes, maybe an hour to keep working while Sherry became "clean and beautiful."

~ ~ ~

As they drove down the highway Mark said, "I'm going to run in and visit my girlfriends." Sherry knew exactly what he meant. He was going to run into the Tavernier Post Office to check with Beth and Theresa to see if they had any mail. Their mail was forwarded to general delivery while they were in Florida. He couldn't help but smile when he thought of the first time he walked in the post office and asked if there was any Special Delivery mail for Mark Daniels, and one of the ladies said, "Honey, there's nothing special about you, you mean general delivery."

Mark climbed back in the car and handed Sherry a stack of envelopes. "Just bills," he said.

The drive was pleasant, bright sunshine out the windshield and a gray threatening sky in the rear view mirror. When Mark parked the car at the Sandal Factory he noticed a jewelry store a few shops down with a sign stating in big bold print, "Shipwreck Treasure!"

"Take your time Sweetie, I'm going down to the jewelry store," he said leaning to the right to read the store's name, "The Treasure Chest." Mark unbuckled his seatbelt and climbed out of the car.

Sherry looked at Mark and said, "Oh, Mark are you going to buy me a sparkly bauble."

"No. I'm doing some research. I want to find out more about Spanish treasure. I have an interest since I found the mystery file."

Mark knew turning Sherry loose in a shoe store and telling her to take her time could be problematic. Shoes were her drug. She loved shoes and since they came down to the Keys her addiction has been focused on sandals.

The salesgirl was assisting a customer when Mark opened the door to the jewelry store and a little bell sounded. The girl acknowledged Mark with a smile and said, "I'll be right with you."

"Take your time, I'm going to look around," Mark told her as he found a glass display case of treasure coins. There were silver coins of all sizes, some wrapped in gold hanging from chains, smaller coins set in rings and still other coins in individual cellophane bags. A sign in the corner of the case read, "All our coins are certified."

Mark leaned over the case looking at the coins and saw several familiar designs from reading about them in the mystery file. He recognized a round coin with a pair of pillars and waves, another with a shield with lions and castles and pomegranate at the bottom. According to the little cards by each coin there were ½, 1, 2, 4 and 8 Real coins.

"Hi, can I help you?" the pretty salesgirl asked as the bell rang signaling her previous customer was leaving the store. "I see you have found our treasure coin collection." Not waiting for Mark to respond she started in on the sales pitch: "All of our coins are verified by a certified assayer, unlike some dealers who sell so called treasure coins. Believe me they are not all real."

"What do you mean, not real?" Mark asked.

"There are people who create counterfeit coins and try to pass them off as authentic, and there are coins that are stamped out of actual shipwreck silver bars but are not coins found on wrecks."

Mark looking at the case asked, "Is that legal?"

"Yes, as long as the consumer is told the coin is a replica stamped in shipwreck silver and not an actual shipwreck coin. They are less expensive but are not actual coins. People bring them in all the time and try to pass them off as real sunken treasure coins. They have value, usually the silver value but no historic coin value. Don't get me wrong, they look good and are more reasonably priced. We sell a bunch of them."

Mark told the woman, "I'm an author and I'm doing some research on the Spanish Treasure Fleet and sunken treasure."

Sensing she was not going to make a sale but intrigued to be a part of a book she says, "I can help you, what do you want to know?"

"I have read a lot about the fleet of 1733, a lot of historical documents about Spanish coins and their recovery but what I am looking for is information about treasure that wasn't recovered back then but is being found these days."

The woman said, "Yeah, there is treasure still being found. In this case are our Atocha coins." She stepped to her right. "These coins are from the Nuestra Senora de Atocha, which sank in 1622. I'm sure you have heard of Mel Fisher, the man in Key West who spent 16 years searching for the treasure of the Atocha. This is part of the cache he discovered."

Mark shook his head in agreement as he looked through the glass at the coins. "Yeah, I toured the Mel Fisher Museum in Key West and there is a lot online about him and the Atocha, but what about other Spanish shipwrecks? Are there any around here in the middle Keys?"

The woman realized she was not dealing with the average tourist, rather a person knowledgeable about sunken treasure and said, "I'm Amber," and reached her hand forward.

"Hi Amber, Mark," he said lightly grasping her hand.

Amber began, "Four ships from the 1733 Spanish Treasure fleet were grounded on the reef north of here, up by Matecumbe. Most of their cargo was recovered over the years but to this day there are still coins that wash up on the beach or are found by divers."

Mark offered, "I read that the guy they found tied to his sunken boat was a treasure hunter."

"Oh, you're talking about Chopper. Yeah he is a legend around here, or was a legend," Amber corrected herself. "The rumor was that he found a lot of stuff on the bottom like silver and gold from the wrecks and some other stuff."

"Like what kind of other stuff?" Mark asked fascinated with Amber's story.

"It's rumored he was bringing in some 'not quite legal' stuff, like square grouper."

"What? Is that a protected fish?" Mark asked knowing a grouper was a fish but not familiar with the square species.

Amber laughed and answered, "Around here bales of marijuana are known as square grouper. Chopper was rumored to have made a few midnight trips out on the ocean and come back with a load or two. And it was also said that he found other illegal cargo on the bottom. You know the kind of stuff tossed off a boat when the Coast Guard got too close."

She continued, "He thought of himself as a pirate. In fact, last Halloween he dressed up as a pirate and kept telling corny jokes; like being a pirate is addictive, when you lose your first hand you get hooked, or saying that he wanted to get his hands on my treasure chest. He was a colorful guy," Amber said with a smile.

She continued, "I work part time at Smugglers, a local bar, and met Chopper there. He was a pretty good guy. When I was at FKCC I did some research on local shipwrecks."

"Where were you?" Mark asked.

"Florida Keys Community College. That was a lifetime ago. But I did research for a paper on the wrecks off Marathon. And I interviewed Chopper."

"Did he tell you anything interesting?"

"He told me that there is still silver on the bottom from the wreck of the *Almiranta* up off Long Key. He said that it carried hundreds of cases of silver. Most was salvaged, but some was buried in the sand and is uncovered now and then. Chopper would go out there and search the bottom after storms to see what was exposed."

"Just the, what did you say, the *Almiranta?*" Mark asked.

"No, one night he was drunk and was telling me that he also searched the wrecks of the *San Francisco, San Pedro and El Tyrri*. All from the 1733 fleet and all up off Matecumbe."

Mark asked, "He would just tell you stuff like that?"

"Well, when he was drinking he liked to talk, or brag about being a pirate. Not so much to the guys at the bar, but to the girls. I found if I let him rest his hand on my thigh he would answer almost anything I asked. He was a nice guy when he was sober but a letch as a drunk."

"Did he ever say anything about finding silver?

"Yeah, sort of. He never came out and said he found treasure but led me to believe he did. I drew the line at the hand on the thigh thing, but I probably would have found out more if I let him lay my head on a pillow."

"I heard that he made a big find and that's what got him killed," Amber said. "I'm going to miss him. He was a dirty old man, but I kind of liked him."

Mark smiled at the girl, a pretty girl, someone who once had dreams of a college education and a future but now sold treasure coins to the tourists. "What do you think he found?"

"It's probably just bar talk, but they say he and the Fuente's may have found a lot of treasure while they were working a salvage job."

"Who are the Fuente's?" Mark asked, his old reporter instincts taking over.

"Enrique and his dad. They work for Chopper. Well, used to work for Chopper. I was going to ask Enrique if it was true, I used to date him, but he hasn't been at the bar for a while."

The little bell on the door rang as a customer entered and Mark thanked Amber for talking with him. She handed him a business card for the store saying, "Call anytime." Mark removed one of his cards from his wallet and handed it to her. Amber started to walk down the counter towards the young couple jewelry shopping, and turned back and said, "Hey Mark, I want a copy of your book when it's published."

"You got it," Mark said, then added, "Amber, hold that dream and go back to school." She smiled back at him.

Mark walked to the car finding that Sherry was still shopping. He thought about going to find her and rescue their poor anemic Visa card but rather he sat in the car and wrote notes from his conversation with Amber.

Sherry walked out with two shopping bags, one definitely holding a shoe box. They went to Burdines for lunch, shopped for furnishings for the condo, then headed back north. Sherry took a call from Mandy and Mark kept the car between the lines and drifted off in thought.

He thought about what Amber had told him about Chopper. Had he found a cache of treasure and been killed for it? Was his death the result of a drug deal? He felt the death of Chopper was definitely connected to something big, and probably illegal. But what?

Chapter 18

Mark and Sherry were relaxing on the beach as they did most days, spending a warm day on the sand while their friends back home in Michigan dug out from the latest blizzard. Sherry was reading a trashy novel and Mark reviewed the notes about Florida shipwreck treasure. Since finding the mystery file, Mark had become preoccupied with the thought of silver and gold coins just lying on the bottom of the ocean waiting to be found.

"Mr. Daniels, may I speak with you for a minute?"

Mark looked up to find a uniformed sheriff's deputy looking at him through dark glasses. "Can I have a word with you about the accident that occurred on US1?"

"Of course, what can I do for you, officer?" Mark said. Through the years of covering crime as a reporter he saw what police officers and sheriff's deputies had to deal with on a daily basis. He had a healthy respect for law enforcement.

Mark and the deputy walked off the beach to the condo where they could talk in private. As they climbed the stairs, Mark could imagine the scene on the beach; people crowding around Sherry asking; "Why did a cop escort Mark off the beach? Has Mark been arrested?" Mark was sure the condo rumor mill was running at full speed.

The deputy was the same officer who took Mark's statement the day of the accident. He was doing some follow up on the accident.

Sargent Radak asked, "Did the victim say anything to you when you got to the car?"

Mark responded, "No."

"Was the victim still alive when you got to him?"

"I don't think so. I felt for a pulse and looked for a sign of him breathing but didn't see any," Mark answered.

The deputy wrote notes in a small notebook then asked, "Was he driving erratically before he struck the power pole?"

"I didn't see him hit the pole," Mark said. "I was in the condo parking lot, heard the crash and ran to the road after the car impacted the pole. Why?"

"Some witnesses reported that he was speeding and driving recklessly, I wondered if you saw that before the accident."

"Sorry I can't help you anymore than what I told you. The accident had already occurred when I got there and the man was unresponsive. He never regained consciousness while I was with him."

"Well, thank you for taking time to meet with me Mr. Daniels. I didn't suspect you had anything more to add but I needed to ask."

The men stood and walked towards the door and Sargent Radak said, "Oh, Mr. Daniels, the wife of the victim asked if she could talk to you. I guess it is a way for her to deal with the grieving process, you know talk to the last person to see her husband alive."

"Yes, of course, I would be happy to talk to her. Give her my phone number if you like."

Chapter 19

Enrique's cell vibrated in his pocket. He was working at Jimmy Tito's auto repair and didn't want to take the call. Jimmy was kind enough to give him a job after Sunshine Marine closed because of Chopper's death and Enrique didn't want to be one of those guys who was on his phone every five minutes. He let it vibrate. It stopped as he was tightening the lug nuts on a white Silverado. Then it started vibrating again. He let it vibrate then it stopped, then it started again.

Thinking it must be something important he wiped the grease from his hands on a red shop towel and pulled out his cell, "Hola."

It was his father practically yelling into the phone, "Papa, slow down, slow down."

Luis Fuentes took a deep breath and said, "The policía come to here, and tell me Roberto is dead. He dead! He murdered!" Luis screamed into the phone. "The policía want know why. Why, Enrique, why Roberto dead? Why people kill Roberto?"

"Papa, I don't know why, but don't say a word about nothing. You know what I'm saying, I mean not a word about nothing!"

Chapter 20

The laptop on his lap, a coffee at his side, Sherry next to him with her morning creamer and caffeine, sitting on the balcony overlooking Florida Bay, Mark was counting his blessings. He stared out over the water, thinking the TV weather lady said it might be a record setting warm day, and according to the weather app on his phone it was 11 degrees with snow expected back home. Life is Good, he thought.

Mark's revelry was interrupted when his cell phone rang. "Hello," Mark answered. "Oh, hello Mrs. Main. Yes, of course, tomorrow works for me. Eleven is fine. Do you need directions? Okay, I'll see you then."

"Who was that you made a date with?" Sherry asked. "Do you want me to leave and give you and your lady friend some quiet time? What do you need, five, ten minutes?" Sherry joked with her husband.

"It was Mrs. Main, the widow of the man who was killed in the accident out on US1. She wants to come by and talk to me," Mark said.

~ ~ ~

"Hello, Mrs. Main. Please come in," Mark greeted the woman at the front door. "I'm Mark Daniels and this is my wife Sherry."

Mark and the forty something year old woman sat on the couch. "I appreciate you agreeing to meet with me," the woman said accepting an iced tea from Sherry. "This has been so upsetting. My life was turned upside down in just 9 days."

"Life is funny. One day I was driving to work mad at Tim for being so involved with something at work that he forgot our anniversary and the next day I was burying him. I'm having a lot of trouble dealing with this. Mr. Daniels. I was wondering if Tim said anything to you before he passed away?"

Mark set his glass of tea on a coaster on the glass top coffee table and answered, "Mrs. Main." She interrupted him, "Please Lynn." Mark began again, "Lynn, your husband was unconscious when I arrived at the car, and he never regained consciousness while I was there."

Mrs. Main thought a moment and said, "The police asked if Tim was taking any kinds of medication or was a heavy drinker. They said he was speeding and driving like a wild man before the accident. Do you know anything about that?"

"No, I didn't see him driving before the accident," Mark answered. "Why was Tim in the Keys?"

"I really don't know; I don't know why he was down here," she answered. "He often came down here on business, but I never paid any attention to his work."

Mark said, "Maybe if you knew who he was going to meet it may shed some light as to why he was speeding to get to the meeting."

Sherry said to the woman, "You can ignore my husband, Mark was an investigative reporter and he is always questioning things."

Mark defended himself, "I was just thinking that if he was speeding to get somewhere maybe it would help to know who he was going to meet."

Lynn Main replied, "No, you're right, I should find out where he was going and who he was going to meet, because Tim driving fast is completely out of character. I always accused him of being pokey. He drove like an old man out on a Sunday afternoon. He was not a reckless driver and he always wore his seat belt."

"Did Tim have an appointment book where he kept track of where he was going and with whom he was meeting?"

"If he did it was at his office. I never saw anything at home," she said.

"You might want to check with his employer and see if they know who he was meeting," Mark added. "Are the police checking into where your husband might have had an appointment?"

"No, they said they didn't have the manpower to continue investigating the accident. They said the medical examiner ruled the cause of death was head trauma as a result of an automobile accident."

As they walked towards the door Mrs. Main thanked Sherry and Mark for taking the time to talk to her.

Mark reminded her to check with her husband's employer as to why he was in the Keys, if it was work related, and to call and let him know. "I am curious."

"Oh, Mr. Daniels, I have already bothered you enough," Mrs. Main said.

Sherry patted the woman on her shoulder and said, "Don't worry about that, Mark loves to check things out that don't quite line up. It's in his genes."

"Thank you," the woman said with tears trickling down her cheek."

Sherry reached for the woman giving her a comforting hug.

The next day Mark and Sherry sat on the balcony sipping their morning brews and Mark asked his wife, "Do you remember what Tim Main's occupation was?"

"No, I'm not sure she said," Sherry answered as she was checking the latest news on Facebook.

"I should have asked. I don't know why I didn't ask. As a reporter I would have gotten all of the details. I must be slipping."

"Just call her and ask," Sherry said.

"I didn't get her phone number either. I can't reach her. She has our number but I didn't get hers. Boy, I am really slipping," Mark said picking up both of their cups. "Do you want a refill?"

"Sure," Sherry answered. Then added, "I want to go get our grandbaby something today. Would you like to take a ride?"

They drove up US1 to the Shell World gift shop. "You already sent her a stuffed animal a few weeks ago," Mark reminded her.

"I know, that was a manatee. Remember I sent her a manatee and a book about manatees and the next day we saw a manatee at our dock? So now I want to send her a stuffed dolphin and a book and maybe we will see dolphins."

Mark listened to his wife's logic then added, "Do me a favor, don't send her a stuffed snake."

Chapter 21

"Papa you gotta make sure you don't talk to nobody about the silver and make sure Mama doesn't tell no one," Enrique said to his father.

"But someone kill Roberto. Why Roberto, he not bad man." Luis mourned his younger brother. "Do you know why they kill Roberto?"

"Papa, I think it's something to do with the silver. Maybe someone Roberto talked to about the coins is trying to steal the treasure. Did you get Roberto's personal effects?"

Luis looks at his son with a confused expression.

Enrique realized his father didn't know what that meant. "Did the police give you the stuff Roberto had on him; his wallet and stuff he had in his pockets?"

"Si," Luis answered.

"Were the coins with it?" Enrique asked.

"No, no coins."

"Did his wallet have money in it?" Enrique asked knowing that Roberto usually didn't have money to put in his wallet.

"No, no wallet."

Enrique thought for a minute then said, "So whoever killed him took the coins."

"Papa, someone is trying to get the silver. First they killed Roberto and Chopper is dead too. I think someone is killing their way to us! Probably torturing them till they tell who has the silver."

"You and Mama have got to hide."

"Where we go?"

"Go up to Miami and visit Aunt Angela, or go see Uncle Alejándro, but get out of town for a while. I'm going to hide too. I'll get in touch with you and let you know when it's safe to come back. You and Mama need to get out of town right away. Not tomorrow, now, before they figure out it is us who have the silver and they come after us too."

"Okay, we go tonight. But, not to Alejándro's house. He don like me and I don like him. He think his sister make mistake marryin me. Maybe we go see Cristóbal and Marissa in Okeechobee. We no see em since before Christmas."

"Good, just go right away. Go tell Mama you have to leave real soon and get out of town. And don't tell anyone where you're going. It's for your safety." Enrique pulled some money from his front pocket and handed it to his father. "Here take this. You're going to need some money to live on. I'll try to send you more when I can."

Chapter 22

Mark sat on the lower balcony of their condo in Tavernier, Florida. It was 7:15 in the morning and already 74 degrees. He thought to himself, "It's going to be another beautiful day". There were only a few fluffy white clouds interspersed in a pure blue sky. There wasn't a hint of wind, the palm trees were motionless and the water of Florida Bay was calm and flat. There was a large iguana lounging in a tree, pelicans perched on the dock pilings and seagulls screeched as they fought over a fish. Mark opened the computer, sipped his coffee while it booted up, and gave thanks for this opportunity to witness God's splendor.

This morning Mark would change up his routine a little. Rather than first checking the Detroit Free Press his curiosity about the guy who was tied to his sunken boat led Mark to go directly to the Florida Keys online newspaper. He wanted to learn all he could about the man named Chopper who was rumored to have found sunken treasure and wound up being murdered in a most unusual way. The story read like a cheap novel, he thought.

There wasn't anything new about Chopper's death, just the same article from yesterday and a summary of finding the body, its recovery and a statement that the Sheriff's Department was investigating Mr. Wirsbinski's death.

Mark wrote in his notebook the information of how Chopper's body was discovered by the glass bottom boat just in case he wanted to use something similar in his Lake of the Ozarks novel. Maybe his protagonist, Will Mellard, could murder someone, tie them to a boat, sink it at a marina and wait for the early morning fishermen to walk the dock and make the gruesome discovery. Maybe this time he'd make the victim a woman. He thought;

The morning sun penetrated the water in shafts of silver shimmering off her long blond hair flowing with the current, her lithe body, Mark thought a moment then made a change ... *her lithe naked body was tied to a boat scuttled in a slip.* "Yeah, I'll make her naked, it sounds more perverse. It sounds like something Will would do, he is a perverted murderer." Mark quickly jotted down notes before he forgot them. He smiled thinking of his creativity in how he came up with dramatic ways to kill people as he returned to the computer and his search for news.

A large powerboat with four 300 HP engines on its stern roared by, Mark heard it before he saw it. The boat racing by on the intercostal waterway was followed by several others. It must be a Poker Run, he thought to himself. I heard they often make runs in these go fast boats from Miami down the intercostal to Key West. In fact, I read in the Keys News there is a Miami to Havana race being organized. That reminded him what he was doing when he got off track; he was reading the Keys newspaper online. He redirected his attention back to the computer screen.

He scanned the headlines about a man arrested on Big Pine for drunk driving on a bicycle, a tourist from Ontario who was arrested for trying to run down the free range chickens on the streets of Key West with a golf cart, and an article about the man found dead near the old missile site in north Key Largo. Mark clicked on that one.

He had read an earlier article about a body being found in the woods. This was a follow up article that summarized the discovery of the body by two tourists but also identified the victim. The dead man was Roberto Luis Fuentes.

Mark read the article with interest because he enjoyed a good murder and this one happened just up the road near the old Cold War missile site. Mark liked it because the location gave it a bit of international intrigue.

Mark was jotting notes about his protagonist, Will Mellard, leaving the body of one of his victims hanging in an abandoned missile silo somewhere in the hills of Missouri, when he said out loud, "Son of a bitch!"

"Roberto Luis Fuentes! Roberto Luis Fuentes," Mark repeated as he frantically flipped pages over the metal spiral of his notebook. He stopped, read and flipped more pages before he found the entry he was looking for, the notes he took after meeting Amber at the jewelry store. He ran his finger down along the margin as his eyes scanned the penciled notes, and stopped at the name Enrique Fuentes.

"Son of a bitch. I wonder if there is a relationship between a guy murdered at the old missile site in north Key Largo and the murder of Chopper sixty or seventy miles away down in Marathon?" Mark flipped to the back cover of the notebook where he had copied the phone number of the jewelry store from the business card Amber gave him.

It was too early to call the store number but he wanted to talk to Amber and see if she knew anything about a guy named Roberto Fuentes and if by chance he was related to the Enrique Fuentes she talked about, the Enrique Fuentes who worked for the other dead man, Chopper. It might be a connection between two seemingly unrelated murders. Mark's reporter instincts were kicking in. However, Mark had no idea where this Roberto Fuentes guy was from. He might be from Miami and dumped in the Keys. I wonder how common the name Fuentes is? Or could he have been somehow related to the guys who were working for Chopper? Were Chopper and Roberto connected to a crime and both murdered by the same people or are they completely unrelated and it's my imagination that is the only connecting factor? Mark began to write himself notes and mumbled, "I'll wait until 10:00 am to call Amber. I bet she will know if this Roberto guy is somehow related to Chopper or the guys who work for him."

As he was staring out at the beautiful blue of the Florida Bay and thinking of the possibilities of the Chopper and Roberto connection, he was startled by Sherry appearing at the balcony and asking where her coffee was.

"I'll get it for you Hon. I was deep in thought about a new revelation possibly connecting two seemingly unrelated murders." Mark got up to get himself a fresh cup of coffee and to mix her morning brew.

By the time he set the steaming mugs down, Sherry was already on the phone with their daughter. She smiled a thank you to him and never stopped talking. Mark checked the time, it was still too early to call Amber, so he settled back, sipped coffee, opened his notebook and began to write about Will Mellard running around the Ozarks murdering people.

Mrs. Dralliw awoke earlier than usual. It was a beautiful summer Lake of the Ozarks day, sunny and warm. She opened the sliding glass door wall and stepped out on the deck. She took in a deep breath, looked up to the blue sky and let the morning sun warm her face. Although she was angry with her husband for not coming home last night from his monthly poker game, the morning was so full of promise of a glorious day she didn't let it bother her. The 53-year-old woman stepped from the deck to the grass near the lake. She loved how the morning dew felt on her bare feet, how the blades of grass tickled her toes. The lake was as flat as glass, only small ripples disturbing its mirror like surface. As she stepped on the dock she noticed small bubbles break the surface in concentric rings. "A fish," she thought. "I wonder if it's a bass, or maybe a crappie." She thought as she walked out the dock pausing occasionally to look down through the clear water. When she saw the source of the bubbles her hands instinctively covered her mouth, holding her robe closed no longer a concern. She closed her eyes and opened them again, her vision was not faulty, she saw what she thought she saw; four men underwater sitting around a table as if they were playing cards. The men were tied to cement blocks, their arms floating out in front of them like zombies. She recognized the men of the submerged poker game; they were her neighbors, Bart, Darrel, Bill and the fourth was her husband Ken.

Mark drew a large X through the section he had just written and said, "No, scratch that. The logistics of Will Mellard killing four men and posing them in the lake in a macabre submerged poker game just didn't work. How could he do it by himself in just one night. Nope, the scenario is too unbelievable."

He took a sip of coffee and looked out over the water searching for something to stimulate his mind. Maybe he could have Will prop up a dead body on a park bench. Mark was jotting down notes about the discovery of a dead body in the Harry Truman State Park, when his cell phone rang bringing him back to reality.

He looked at the screen, but he didn't recognize the number. He thought twice about answering then curiosity got the best of him, "Hello," he said.

"Hello, Mark?" a female voice asked on the other end of the line.

"Yes, this is Mark," he replied, mentally preparing for the woman to try to sell him something

"Mark, I don't know if you remember me but this is Amber. We were talking the other day at the Treasure Chest in Marathon. I hope you don't mind me calling but I have to talk to you."

"Amber, of course I remember you. It's nice to hear from you, in fact I was going to call you in a while. What can I do for you?"

"I have some new information about pirate coins, I mean treasure coins. Sorry, the tourists like to think the coins are part of a pirate's booty. Remember I was telling you that I used to date Enrique Fuentes and he worked for Chopper, and that I haven't seen Enrique for a while? Well I wasn't exactly telling the truth. I have talked to him. And now I need to talk to someone. I thought about you and did a search and the Internet says you are a reporter."

"I'm a retired reporter," Mark interjected.

"Yeah, a retired reporter but you were a good one. You wrote about all the big stuff, like Jimmy Hoffa and you won a bunch of awards and shit. Oops, sorry about that. From what I read on Google you sound like a good person, someone who I can trust."

"Not a problem. How can I help you?"

"Well," Amber hesitated. "Well, like, the police are looking for Enrique. They think he killed Chopper, but he didn't. He said he didn't even know Chopper was dead until he heard it on the radio. And now his uncle is dead. Did you hear about the body found up in Key Largo? That was Enrique's uncle. Someone murdered him and left him for the snakes and rats to eat. Mark, I'm scared," she said all without taking a breath.

I thought there was a relation between the dead guy in Key Largo and the dead guy in Marathon, Mark thought. "Amber, slow down. Do you know where Enrique is?"

There wasn't a response.

"Amber?" Mark said.

"Yeah, I'm here. Yeah, I know where Enrique is. He's staying at my house. But Mark, please don't tell anyone. He is really afraid. The police are searching for him and he is afraid the guys who murdered Chopper and Roberto are after him too."

"Why would they be after him?" Mark asked.

"He won't say but I think he got messed up in some bad stuff with Chopper, you know, smuggling or stealing, or something. I think they may have got involved with some bad people."

Mark asked, "What does his uncle have to do with all of this?"

"I don't know. Maybe he is involved too. Enrique wouldn't say. He said the less I know the better off I am. But Mark I'm scared and I didn't have anyone to turn to, that's why I called you. I don't know what to do. I can't go to the police because they are after Enrique. Mark what should I do?"

Mark thought to himself that he shouldn't get involved. He should just wish her well and hang up. But, he couldn't, maybe it was the reporter in him, maybe it was the two intriguing murders, maybe it was the whole pretty damsel in distress thing, but he couldn't just dismiss Amber. He had to at least listen to her.

"Okay, Amber, start from the beginning."

Chapter 23

Sitting on their balcony, Sherry talked with their daughter and Mark listened to Amber as he wrote notes in his notebook. He could hear the worry, concern and fear in her voice as she told Mark what she knew.

"Enrique called me the other day about midnight and asked if I could pick him up. He asked if he could hang out with me for a few days because he lost his job at Sunshine Marine when Chopper got killed and he couldn't pay his rent. He figured the landlord probably had called the police to have him evicted so he didn't want to go back to his place.

We had a few beers and Enrique began to talk. He told me that he didn't know anything about Chopper getting murdered, but he heard the police think he did it."

"Why would they think that?" Mark asked.

"He said they think Chopper caught him stealing or something and Enrique killed him to cover it up. But he says he didn't steal from Chopper. If anything, Chopper was the one stealing; you know, paying them under the table not reporting their hours to the government so he wouldn't have to pay unemployment and taxes. The old pirate wasn't exactly a candidate for the Chamber of Commerce Man of the Year Award, if you know what I mean."

Mark noticed that Amber seemed to be relaxing as she talked. She wasn't quite as frantic as she was when she first called.

Mark asked, "Amber I think that Enrique needs to get out of Marathon. It's a small island, he is sure to be found and that would mean you being arrested for harboring a criminal."

Amber gave a slight laugh and said, "I don't live in Marathon. He is with me at my house in Islamorada."

"Oh, I guess I just assumed you lived in Marathon," Mark said, a little ticked at himself for assuming. "You have quite a drive to work."

"Yeah, 23.7 miles each way," Amber said.

"Well, it's good that you're not in Marathon, anyway," Mark said.

"Mark I've got to get ready for work. Do you mind if I call you later when I'm driving to the store? I'll probably be sitting in traffic anyway. Sometimes it takes me over an hour to drive those 23.7 miles."

"Sure Amber. No problem, I'll be here," Mark said then heard her click off on the other end. He thought for a moment then said, "What am I getting myself into."

Mark sat looking out over the water and thought. "Why am I drawn to these kind of situations? Is it the reporter in me, my natural inquisitiveness? Is it the unique way Chopper was killed? Is it the mysterious and related deaths of Chopper and Roberto? Heck, it might just be because Amber is such a pretty girl and I enjoy talking to her."

To take his mind off the whole Amber, Enrique, Chopper, Roberto deal, Mark opened his notebook to review what he had recently written about his serial killer stalking the people of the Lake of the Ozarks.

"Maybe I should turn it into a serial killer who preys on people at popular vacation spots throughout the United States. It would expand the amount and variety of people Will Mellard can murder. It could become a travelogue of exciting destinations with a few murders thrown in. National Parks, monuments, famous cities, the possibilities are endless. Hell, Death Valley could take on a whole new meaning. The answer to the old joke of who is buried in Grant's tomb might change, South Dakota's Badlands has potential and I'll bet I can make people really remember the Alamo. This has so much potential maybe I'll write it as a separate book and call it *Natural Beauty/Unnatural Death.*"

Mark quickly wrote the name down in his notes before he forgot it. "I think I can have some fun with this idea," He muttered aloud.

"What?" Sherry asked.

"Oh, nothing just thinking of the next book."

"Next book?" Sherry questioned. "Don't you think you should finish the first book first?"

The ringing of Mark's cell phone saved him from having to explain himself to his wife. "Hello?" Mark answered then said, "Hi Amber."

Mark held the phone to his ear with his shoulder as he flipped pages of his notebook and picked up his pencil.

He listened and took notes and finally interrupted Amber and asked, "Amber, what do you expect of me?"

"I don't know. I'm scared. I'm worried. I'm concerned for Enrique. I don't know what to do. Mark, what should I do?"

"I really don't know," Mark said honestly. "I won't know until I talk to Enrique. Do you think he will open up to me?"

"I don't really know. I'm not sure he has been completely open with me and I'm sleeping with the guy. But maybe if he talks with you and realizes you are on his side he will be open and honest with you. No guarantees though. Do you think we can get together and talk?"

"I don't want to get involved unless he will talk with me. I can't help unless he is open and honest with me," Mark said.

"Thanks Mark. I think you are his only chance. You have nothing to gain and nothing to lose by helping him. Hopefully he will see it that way and we can work our way through this mess. Well I just turned into the parking lot at Treasure Chest. I gotta go, I'm late for work."

"Amber call me tonight. Let me talk to Enrique. Maybe I can convince him to tell me what's going on with the murders of Roberto and Chopper. And what it means for him."

"I'll try to talk him into talking with you, but I don't know. I'll call you tonight when I get home."

"Okay, I'll be waiting for your call. And Amber, stay safe, I don't want to see you get hurt," Mark added in what he hoped would be taken in a fatherly way.

Chapter 24

The day continued like most days. Sherry and Mark enjoyed the morning on the balcony then lounged on the beach with friends. Sherry explored Facebook, read magazines and a book on her Kindle and talked with Mandy while Mark reviewed the notes about his conversation with Amber. He wrote out questions that he would ask Enrique, and what he suspected about Enrique's involvement with the gruesome murders of Roberto and Chopper.

While Sherry prepared dinner Mark stared at the news program on the television but was thinking about Amber and Enrique. "Could Enrique have possibly killed both Chopper and his uncle? Maybe Chopper had Roberto murdered and then the killers killed Chopper. Or what about Enrique's father? Where is he in all of this. He worked for Chopper too but Amber hadn't mentioned a word about him. Maybe the dad killed his boss and brother." Mark knew a lot of the thoughts were probably nonsense but he had to consider all possibilities.

His thoughts were put on hold when his cell phone rang. "Hello?" he said without looking at the caller ID. He was expecting Amber to call and he was surprised to find Mrs. Main on the line.

"Mr. Daniels, you told me to call when I found out why Tim was going down to the Keys. I checked with his employer and all they could say was that he was going to meet with someone in Marathon about Spanish coins."

"What?" Mark practically yelled into the phone. "I'm sorry, but what did you say?"

Lynn Main told Mark that her husband worked as a marine archaeologist for Undersea Archaeology of Miami. She continued, "He was going to meet with a man named Roberto Fuentes about some silver coins he brought to the company to be certified." Mark's head was spinning with questions and the unique relationship between all of what had been occupying his mind for the last several days. Now he learned that the horrible accident that killed Tim Main might be central to the murders of Roberto and Chopper.

Mark thanked Mrs. Main for calling and he got her phone number for future reference. He hung up as Sherry said, "Dinner is ready."

"Son of a bitch!" Mark said.

Sherry picked up the bowl of pasta she had just placed on the table and said playfully, "If that's your attitude, get your own dinner."

Mark ate in silence, reviewing in his mind the new development.

"Where are you?" Sherry asked. "I asked you if you minded if I went to lunch with the girls tomorrow and you just ignored me. Did you even hear me?"

Deep in thought, Mark put his fork down and walked to his desk. He withdrew the mystery file saying, "Son of a bitch."

"What is wrong with you?" Sherry asked.

"The file. The mystery file, I bet it belongs to Tim Main. When I opened the door to the car I tossed my notebook and file on the car seat. I bet when I grabbed my stuff I also grabbed this file from the car, one of Mr. Main's files about Spanish coins and shipwrecks." Mark turned the file over pointing to what looked like chocolate brown fingerprints. He placed his fingers on the stain. "When I moved his head off the steering wheel I got blood on my hand and this is probably his blood. The file was in the car. The mystery of the mystery file is solved!"

Chapter 25

That night Mark lay awake watching the ceiling fan spin as Sherry lightly snored. He ran all of the facts through his mind. Tim Main crashed his car into a power pole on US1 outside his condominium. Mr. Main was said to be speeding and driving recklessly. Mr. Main was on his way to see Roberto Fuentes. Roberto Fuentes was murdered. Roberto's brother and nephew both worked for Chopper. Chopper was murdered, found tied to his sunken boat. Those were the facts; those were undisputed; they were all connected, but what Mark couldn't figure out was the why.

Why were the two men murdered and why was Tim Main driving erratically and ultimately lost control and crashed into the pole? Was he being chased? Was he a victim of the pirates who killed Roberto and Chopper trying to get their treasure? Mark didn't like the thought, but there was nothing that excluded Enrique from being the killer. He could still be the person behind the deaths and Amber's life could be in danger. Or maybe Amber was in on it too. Maybe she and Enrique are the killers and for some reason I'm being dragged into their web of deceit.

"No, I don't think Amber could be involved. She seemed genuinely scared. And why would she include me in this if she were involved in the murder of two men. You would think a murderer would want less people involved, especially an experienced investigative reporter. I think I would be the last person I would talk too if I were a murderer. I've got to quit thinking about this and get some sleep."

The next morning Mark had to forgo his usual perch on the balcony; rather, he was sitting on the couch staring out the sliding glass door at the rain. The palms were bent in the wind, the sky was an angry gray, the rain came in a heavy downpour and he couldn't believe Sherry was sleeping through the loud rolling thunder. Mark smiled, thinking that even paradise needed to turn ugly now and then to make the flowers bloom, the trees grow and to keep the islands in their lush tropical splendor.

He picked up his notebook and flipped through the pages refreshing his memory of the whole mess he had become immersed in. He was jotting down his last night's sleepless thoughts when his cell rang. He looked at the time; 7:45, then the caller ID: Amber.

"Good Morning Amber," Mark said probably too cheerfully on this dreary day. "Is it raining down your way?"

"Yeah, its pouring. I'm driving to work and the traffic is terrible. The storm, and the fact that it's a Saturday during peak tourist season results in a very slow commute for me."

"Hey Mark, I talked to Enrique last night about you and he said there was no way in hell he would talk to some stranger and he was pissed I told you that he was staying with me. He was yelling and throwing a total fit."

Mark asked, "Amber do you think Enrique might harm you in anyway? Maybe you need to get away from him."

"Naw, he really is a gentle guy. I think he is scared. He is afraid of being caught and afraid of whoever killed his uncle and Chopper. I'm alright, but thanks for your concern, it's sweet. If you meet Enrique, you'll see that he is a nice guy caught up in a bad situation. You know like they say on Bloodlines, that TV show filmed in the Keys, *"We're not bad people, but we did a bad thing."* That's Enrique," Amber said, "He is not a bad guy, but I think he may have done something bad."

"Amber, you haven't said anything about Enrique's father. Where is he in all of this?" Mark asked as he reached for a pencil to record her answer if it was pertinent.

"Enrique said his mom and dad decided to take a vacation. Mark, that's not like his dad at all. In all the time I've known Enrique I never heard of his dad even leaving the islands. That doesn't make a lot of sense. Do you think he's okay? I mean, with everyone getting killed I hope Luis is okay."

"I hope so too," Mark said. "You should check with Enrique. Do you think he will meet with me?"

Amber sighed and said, "I don't know. I'll keep working on him. He needs to do something. All he does is sit and watch TV, drink beer and worry."

"Hey Mark, thanks for talking with me. I needed to talk to someone before this whole thing drove me nuts. I'm getting another call so I'll talk with ya later," Amber said and hung up.

Mark heard Sherry stirring upstairs and got up to refresh his coffee and make Sherry her morning potion. As he poured the French vanilla into her cup, Mark thought of Amber and what she was going through. She was selling the tourists tourist crap and worked as a part time bar tender. He thought: It's a shame that young people need to work two jobs or more just to live in paradise. The Keys derives its livelihood from the millions of tourists who vacation there, and the tourism drives the cost of living on the islands up. But the tourism industry requires a lot of people to serve the drinks and dinners, clean the hotel rooms, and maintain the landscape, but those jobs tend to be low paying jobs. And the people who serve the tourists need to work two or more jobs to just to pay rent and eat. It's a screwed up economy.

Mark worried about Amber. He worried that she was involved in the suspicious death of two men. He worried that the man Amber was currently living with was the man who killed the two men, or possibly three if Tim Main was indeed murdered by the same person. He worried that Amber might be in danger but too trusting to be aware of the threat. Mark also wondered why the hell he got involved in this in the first place.

Mark's cell rang. It was Amber. "Mark, its Amber. That was Enrique who called and he says he will meet with you but he isn't sure he will talk to you until he is positive you are okay."

"That's great Amber, Where and when?"

"He said he doesn't trust you and he doesn't want you to know where we are living, so he agreed to meet you in a public place away from my house. How about the Mile Marker 88 beach bar? We can be there at 7:00 tonight if that works for you? Do you know where it is?"

"Ah yeah, at mile marker 88," Mark answered then said, "Seven tonight will work,"

"Oh and Mark, Enrique wants you to come alone."

"No problem. I'll be there by myself."

"Okay, gotta go," Amber said and hung up.

Mark turned to Sherry and said, "Honey, I've got to tell you what is going on."

Chapter 26

Mark parked in the crushed coral parking lot of the Mile Marker 88 beach bar which was located at, where else but mile marker 88 along US1. The hostess escorted him to a table near the water and he ordered a Hurricane Hole, his favorite beer from the Florida Keys Brewing Company.

While he waited for Amber and Enrique to arrive, Mark sipped his beer and watched a couple attempting to dock their boat at the restaurant pier. They first pulled alongside the pier and cut the engines and the offshore breeze blew them away from the dock before they could get a line to the cleat. They powered up and took another try at docking. This time he over compensated and ran the bow hard into a piling. He backed off and circled back to try it again. Mark was enjoying the entertainment when Amber arrived at the table.

Mark stood and Amber greeted him with a hug. Looking over her shoulder for Enrique, Mark asked, "Where is he?"

The waiter appeared and Amber ordered another Florida Keys brew, a Honey Bottomed Blonde and began to explain, "I don't know. I came home and he was gone. He hasn't left the house in days and now he is gone. I drove around looking for him but nothing."

"Did you call his cell phone?" Mark asked.

"Yes, that was the first thing I did, but when I called it rang in the bedroom. He didn't take it with him."

"Amber, did he take his clothes, like he was moving out?"

"No. As far as I know everything is still there; clothes, cell, wallet, keys, it's all still at my house. I'm worried. Do you think someone took him?"

Mark took a drink of his beer as he thought then asked, "Did it look like anyone broke into the house? I mean was there any damage, were there things out of place?"

"No, nothing I noticed. It looked just like it did in the morning when I left for work. You might look at my house and think the place had been ransacked but it's the way it usually looks. I'm not exactly Suzie Homemaker."

"Does Enrique have a car?"

"He has an old pickup truck but it is in Marathon," Amber answered.

"How did he get to your house?" Mark asked.

"He called me and I picked him up."

"Did he ever leave the house?"

"No, well yeah, he borrowed my car the day after I picked him up. He said he had to pick up some stuff."

Mark glanced out at the pier and noticed the boat trying to dock was gone. Mark thought, "They must have given up." He returned his thoughts to Amber, "You said he called you at work, what did he say?"

"I called him a couple of times and begged him to meet with you. He finally agreed to meet here and that was the last I heard from him. It was probably around 2:30 or 3:00."

"Do you think the police found him and arrested him?" Mark asked.

"No, I don't think so. These islands are small, news travels fast. I would have heard if Enrique was arrested. I really don't think so."

"Amber, since there is no sign of forced entry, maybe Enrique just walked away. Maybe he decided to leave before whoever killed his boss and uncle came looking for him. Maybe he left to protect you. You know, making sure the pirates didn't find him in your house and put your life in jeopardy too."

Amber lifted her bottle and drained it then said, "Yeah, maybe. But you would think he would at least say goodbye.

"Do you feel safe at your house? Do you think maybe you should find somewhere else to stay for a while? I don't want to see anything bad happen to you."

Amber reached across the table and placed her hand on his and said, "Mark you're sweet to worry about me but I've been on my own for a long time and living down here in the islands a girl grows tough. I'll be alright."

Amber and Mark walked to the parking lot and promised to stay in touch. Mark insisted Amber call him every day to make sure she was all right and to let him know if Enrique showed up. Amber hugged Mark and promised to stay in touch.

Mark drove back to the condo thinking of his conversation with Amber. He had a real concern that something bad had happened to Enrique. He didn't tell Amber, he didn't want to alarm her but why would a man who is wanted by the police and possibly being chased by a murderer leave without his phone, clothes and his identification. Mark thought it pointed to the fact that Enrique didn't leave Amber's house of his own accord. He was probably abducted by the people after the treasure, the pirates.

"Or," Mark said to himself out loud, "maybe he is the guilty party. Maybe he did murder Chopper and his uncle and he has found another hiding place, moved on to someone else to put him up, or maybe he had left the islands all together."

Over their morning concoctions Mark told Sherry about his meeting with Amber. She asked, "Mark, shouldn't you go to the police?"

"I thought about it. But what would I tell them; that the murders of Chopper and Roberto are related? I'm sure they already know that. Tell them that Enrique is in hiding? They know that too. I suppose I could tell them that it is possible the death of Tim Main might be related to the murders, but then I'm not convinced that's true." Mark held his coffee cup in two hands and blew across the hot liquid staring out at Florida Bay and said, "I guess I really don't know much."

Chapter 27

The Florida Keys are a beautiful place to live, but it is an expensive area as well. Many people travel to the Keys from all over the world and try to make a life in the land of sun and fun. Some find jobs and squeak out an existence, some stay until their finances run out then return home with stories of life in paradise, some of questionable mental capability and others heavily involved in alcohol and drugs become homeless.

Many of the homeless wander the streets of Key West and other islands of the Keys. They while away their time on the beaches, in city parks, in the air conditioning of the public libraries and panhandle from the tourists. Many live in the county supported homeless shelters, some sleep in the parks or in the mangroves and some choose to live beneath the bridges along US1.

Through the length of the Florida Keys there is one main road, US1, with over 40 bridges connecting the string of islands. Millions of vehicles cross the bridges carrying commercial, local and tourist traffic. Very few travelers realize that below the roadbed live some of the homeless of the Keys.

Below the Tavernier Creek Bridge between the communities of Tavernier and Islamorada a man lives in an enclosure made of cardboard boxes. The man only leaves his compound after dark, the rest of the time he is huddled in his cardboard house sitting with the hood of his sweatshirt up shielding his face from the boats passing under the bridge.

He sits and stares up and down stream watching the boats parade by; fishing boats, kayaks, paddle boards, and pleasure boats. When the Monroe county Sherriff's or the Florida Fish and Wildlife Commission boats pass by he ducks down low out of sight...

Enrique was in hiding and didn't want to be found.

Chapter 28

"Mark!" Amber screamed into the phone not waiting for Mark's hello. "Mark, Luis Fuentes is dead! Enrique's dad, he's dead!"

"Amber, slow down and tell me what happened."

"Enrique's phone was ringing; did I tell you his phone is here. Anyway his phone rang and I answered it. It was Enrique's mother. She said, who is this, this is Enrique's phone, yes?"

"I told her who I was and told her that Enrique wasn't here but he forgot his phone at my house. She was crying and told me to tell Enrique to call her. She said to tell him that she was coming back to the Keys, back to their house. That Luis was dead."

"How did he die?" Mark asked.

"I don't know. All she said was that Luis was dead and hung up. Mark, this means that Chopper, Roberto and now Luis are dead. What is going on? I mean this is getting scary."

"Amber, I think it has something to do with Spanish coins. Remember that is how we met, I was in your store asking about silver coins. Well, I think they found some treasure. I didn't tell you but there was another man killed that I suspect might be somehow related to the deaths of Chopper and Roberto. He was a marine archaeologist driving down to Marathon to report back to a client there about some coins they discovered, although he was killed in a traffic accident on the way. The man he was going to meet was Roberto."

Amber was quiet for a moment then said, "You know you may be right. One night in bed after a few beers Enrique was telling me that he was going to be rich and telling me that he was going to buy a house and boat and he was going to buy me a new car. I thought he was just talking, you know like people dream about hitting the lottery. Maybe Enrique, Chopper, Roberto and Luis found a stash of treasure."

"Yeah," Mark added, "and they might have contacted the marine archaeologist to have it verified, and it got him killed too."

"Mark, what do I do about Enrique and his dad? His mom thinks I'm going to tell Enrique to go to his parents' home to console his mother, but I don't know where he is or how to get ahold of him."

"Amber, you can't do anything about it but wait for him to contact you," Mark said. "But see if you can find out how Luis died. Was he tortured and murdered like the rest of them?"

Mark clicked off and sat looking out the door-wall. "Two men murdered, a third killed in a car crash, Luis makes a fourth death and Enrique is missing and might be dead. Central to all of the deaths seems to be the rumor of sunken treasure they may have discovered. And now modern day pirates are trying to steal it from them. What have I gotten myself into? I'm not going to investigate any further. My involvement in this mess stops right now. Enrique is gone so Amber should be alright, I'm sure the sheriff's office has figured out the connection between the dead guys and they don't need me butting in. And, I don't want anyone paying an unannounced visit here to Sherry and I."

Mark tried to get his life back to normal. He rose early, sat on the balcony re-reading what he had written about the serial killer stalking the Lake of the Ozarks. Sherry came down a couple of hours later and was checking Facebook and sipping her creamer and coffee, although Mark's mind kept drifting back to Amber and the whole mess. He wondered where Enrique disappeared to and did he do it voluntarily. He wondered if Amber was as innocent in this mess as she professed to be. He wanted to know how Luis Fuentes died; was he tortured and murdered like the others? Mark reviewed the facts of the death of Tim Main and his possible involvement in all of this. Mark did not want to get any more involved than he already was, but then he was very curious to follow it to an end so he decided to follow it from a distance.

His mind made up to ease himself away from the murders. Mark felt a load lifted off his back. He took a drink of coffee as his phone rang. He looked at the caller ID; it was Amber. He let it ring.

Twenty minutes later his phone rang again, interrupting him from writing about Will Mellard killing a loud mouth, know it all, pain in the ass rich guy who had a large boat and a big house on the lake. Will didn't even know the guy, he just didn't like him. But the guy was now just a pile of bloody pieces after going through a commercial wood chipper.

Mark looked and saw it was Amber. Curiosity or journalistic inquisitiveness got the best of him and he answered, "Hi Amber."

"Hey Mark. I found out how Enrique's dad died. A guy came in the store who I know and told me. He is a mate on a crab boat and he always stinks when he comes in off the boat. I think he likes me because he is always stopping by the store and he hangs out at Smugglers."

Mark interrupted Amber, "Amber, What about Luis?"

"Oh yeah. Sorry I got off track. Anyway, Grant, that's the guy I was telling you about, the guy who works on a crab boat, Grant said that he heard that Luis died of a heart attack. He heard that from the captain of his boat who is married to Patty who is a niece of Larry Skinner, who is married to Sandra who is a friend of Mrs. Fuentes so it must be true."

"I hope it's true," Mark said. "If he died of natural causes then he wasn't tortured like the rest of them. Have you heard from Enrique?"

"No, nothing. I'm afraid he's going to miss his father's funeral. But there isn't anything I can do about that, is there?" Amber said.

Mark asked, "So there will be a funeral? I wonder if Enrique will show up if he hears about it. Amber call me if you hear any details."

"Yeah, I gotta go. A couple of customers just walked in." And she hung up.

Mark got up to refresh his coffee and Sherry's concoction as well. As he filled their cups he thought about Luis. He was happy to hear he died of a heart attack, not really happy but happy he wasn't murdered like the rest of them. Chopper and Roberto were obviously murdered and Tim Main might have been too.

Mark heard the distinctive ring of Sherry's cell phone and figured it was their daughter. He set their cups on the small table separating their balcony chairs and Sherry asked, "You don't mind if I go out to lunch today, do you? Bill, Darrel and Mel are going golfing and the women are going to lunch." Mark was not a golfer. He tried the game several time but all he did was lose his balls.

"No. Of course not. I have plenty to do," Mark said as his cell phone rang. It was Amber.

Wanting time to digest what she told him about Luis, he decided not to answer, but on the fifth ring interest got the best of him and he answered. "Hi Amber. Wait, slow down. Start over."

Chapter 29

"Mark, two guys came into the store shopping for treasure coins. They said they were down from Indiana and wanted a keepsake to remember their time in the Keys."

Mark thought: Nothing unusual there.

Amber continued, "They were asking questions about the coins in the case, like where they came from. Then they asked if any of the coins were found locally. Then they asked about Chopper and if I knew if he found any coins. I played dumb, didn't tell them anything. The tall one said he heard that I used to date Enrique and figured I might know. I was getting scared. I just said I didn't know who he was talking about. A woman came in the store and the guys left. I was never so happy to see the woman. She is a regular customer, kind of a rich bitch pain in the ass, but I was never so happy to see her walk in."

"Mark, what do you think? Am I just a nervous Nelly and jumping at shadows? God, that is what my granny used to say. I mean, what do you think about the guys? Do you think they were just tourists like they said and maybe read the newspaper about Chopper?"

"Amber, I don't think they are tourists. How would a tourist from Indiana know that you dated Enrique? Amber you be careful. Did you get a look at their car?"

"Yeah, I watched them walk to the parking lot and they got into a big black SUV and it had tinted windows. I tried to get the license plate number but I couldn't see it."

Mark did his best to calm Amber, but he was concerned for her. Those guys were most likely not tourists in town for the fishing, rather it sounded like they were in the store fishing for information.

Since Sherry was out with friends, Mark could eat anything he wanted. He didn't have to dine on one of her healthy salads, so he walked to the Dairy Queen and got himself a bacon double cheeseburger. Mark sat on the balcony eating his lunch, enjoying the decadent sandwich, feeling his arteries clog with each bite.

As he sipped his diet coke, he heard a knock at the door. It was a man, clean cut and well dressed. He introduced himself as Roger Redmond of the Miramar Mutual Insurance Company. The man explained that he wanted to ask Mark some questions about the accident that occurred in front of the condo.

"Not a problem," Mark said and invited the man in.

They sat on the couch and Mark offered the man a glass of iced tea. The man declined the hospitality and opened a leather bound notebook saying he was investigating a claim made by the deceased man's wife. "There aren't any problems, it's just routine," the man explained.

Some of the questions were the same Mark had answered many other times; "What did Mr. Main say before he died. Was Mr. Main alive when Mark arrived at the scene? Did Mark see Mr. Main driving erratically? Did he seem impaired in any way?"

Mr. Redmond then asked questions that no one else had asked, not the police and not Mrs. Main;

"What was in the car? Was there a briefcase or any kind of bag? Did Mark remove anything from the car?"

Mark became uncomfortable with this line of questioning. It was more of an interrogation than routine insurance questions and Mark asked, "Why are you asking me these type of questions? Is there something missing? Are you accusing me of something?"

"No, no, it's just all routine," Mr. Redmond said.

Mark rose, signaling to the man it was time to leave. "I don't remember anything else that might help you Mr. Redmond. Why don't you give me your business card and if I think of anything I'll give you a call."

The man stood and reached for the pocket of his shirt and said, "Oh, I must have left them in my car. I'll go down and get you a card."

Mark offered, "I'll walk you down and get it so you don't need to climb the stairs again."

"Oh that's alright, I'll be right back."

From the screen door Mark watched the man descend the center stairway and walk to a car where a taller man stood smoking a cigarette. Mr. Redmond opened the door, they both got in, and the car backed out and drove off.

"Shit!" Mark exclaimed. The car was a black Ford Explorer with tinted windows.

Chapter 30

"**A**mber call me as soon as you can!" Mark said into his phone. He wanted to discuss and compare notes on the men who visited her at the store and the man who was at his condo. But she didn't answer so he left a message.

Mark sat back and mentally reviewed the situation as he did when he was a reporter: Were they the same men? Who were they? Were they from the insurance company, like they claimed? Is it possible they really are visitors from Indiana? Were they the murderers who killed 2 or 3 people? If so, what did they want? How did they find me? Are Amber and I in danger? Or, Mark wondered, Is it my overactive imagination working overtime?

Mark began to berate himself: Why didn't I ask him for identification before I let him in the door? I know better than that. What did I tell him? Did I say anything that might be helpful to a murderer? Heck, I don't really know anything that could help the bad guys. Why were they asking if I took anything from Mr. Main's car? Was there anything of value in the car? Did Main have treasure coins with him when he had the accident? That's what he worked on at Undersea Archaeology. His wife said he was going to Marathon to meet with Roberto. Roberto must have found treasure and contacted Mr. Main to verify and certify the coins."

"There are just too many unanswered questions," Mark thought as he stared out at the water. His thoughts were interrupted when his cell phone rang.

"Hey Mark, its Amber. You called?"

"Yes, I just had a visit from an insurance investigator. He was asking questions about the man who died in the car accident out front here."

"Yeah, so?" Amber asked.

"He asked a lot of questions. And he asked if I took anything from the car."

"Did you?"

"No. Well, yes I inadvertently took a file but why did he ask?" Mark wondered. "Oh, and I watched the guy drive away and he was driving a black Ford Explorer with tinted windows."

"No shit!" Amber said. "That is the same car that came to see me at the store saying they were tourists from Idaho or Illinois. One of those "I" states."

"Indiana," Mark said, "You said the guys you talked to were from Indiana."

"Yeah, Indiana. So what the hell? What do they want with us? Do you think they're the guys who murdered Chopper and Roberto?"

Mark responded, "I don't know, but I think we need to be very cautious of black SUV's."

"Mark, I'm scared. I mean these guys found us. How did they know we even know each other?" Amber asked.

"I'm not sure they know that we know each other. Maybe they came to see you because of your connection with Enrique and his connection with Chopper. And they came to question me because of the guy killed in the car crash. Maybe they haven't made a connection between you and I."

Amber listened to Mark then said, "I don't know. This is getting pretty scary if you ask me."

"Amber, have you heard anything from Enrique?"

"No, not a thing. Mark, do you think they found him and have him?"

"Maybe, I don't know. You be careful. Be observant of your surroundings. If anything seems strange or out of the ordinary go to a police station or someplace where there are a lot of people. Be careful!" Mark warned her.

Chapter 31

Enrique's cardboard house provided a hiding place but did little to protect him from the oppressive heat and bugs. He had left Amber's house and moved under the bridge to protect her. Enrique was afraid whoever was after him and killing those around him would find him at Amber's and take it out on her. Enrique decided he would take up residence under the bridge until things settled down.

Enrique called his old friend, Boudro LaFramboise for help. He knew Boudro would help him. They had been friends since Boudro's family moved to the Keys from Louisiana. After high school the boys went different directions; Enrique went to work and Boudro went up to Miami to go to a community college. Enrique learned to repair cars and Boudro learned to repair copy machines.

Enrique asked Boudro to pick him up at Amber's house in lower Matacumbe and give him a ride to Key Largo. Enrique slumped down low in the car as Boudro parked at the Publix grocery store and went in with Enrique's shopping list of several cans of chili, black beans, Spaghetti O's, plantains, potato chips, and toilet paper. Boudro picked out a fishing rod from the selection at the grocery store and grabbed a container of bait then they drove around behind the store and found empty cardboard boxes.

Under the cover of darkness Boudro dropped Enrique and his supplies off near the Tavernier Creek bridge and Enrique took up his new residence beneath the roadbed of US1. At first he was apprehensive of being discovered but after a few days he became comfortable with his new surroundings. He could fish at night and sometime leave the confines of his cardboard bunker to walk in the cool night air without being recognized. After a few days he realized he had to start rationing his food or it wouldn't last until Boudro came by to replenish the supply.

One morning a man surprised Enrique by walking up to his shelter under the bridge. The man, unshaven, and disheveled, told Enrique he would have to leave, that was where he lived. After a few minutes of arguing Enrique realized the man was disturbed and reasoning or being logical with him would not work. So Enrique explained that the department of Homeland Security asked him to stay there to make sure no one tried to blow up the bridge. "You don't want to screw around with the government, now do you?" Enrique asked the man.

"No, I don't want to mess with 'em, thems mean fuckers. You mean the government set you up here?"

"Yup. The orders came straight from the president himself," Enrique answered.

"No wonder you got the good cardboard. Man you got a good house."

"Now you move on and make sure you don't tell no one about this government base down here. We don't want noone getting hurt."

"Oh no man, I ain't gonna tell nobody. I don't wanna mess with no government people, thems mean fuckers. Hey, don't tell them that I was here, will ya. I don't want no trouble."

The man walked off down the creek and Enrique ducked down below the level of his cardboard walls. He had been standing talking with the man while boats went by and hoped no one recognized him. If anyone saw them at all up under the roadbed they probably just saw two homeless guys talking, one in an old dirty tee shirt and the other in a hooded sweatshirt that pretty well covered his face.

Enrique adapted to life under the bridge. The worst was that there wasn't a breeze so it got hot in the day and he got used to the sound of the cars driving above him. The firetrucks with their sirens blaring and the semi-trucks were pretty noisy but he figured he could put up with life under the bridge for a few weeks because when everything settled out he and his dad were going to cash in the silver and be rich.

~ ~ ~

Boudro walked out of the Islamorada Library carrying his tool case. It was the third time he had been called in to fix the copy machine that month. Sitting in the air conditioning of his company car he typed into his laptop a report of what he did to repair the machine; including labor and parts to be billed. Then he made the recommendation that the library copy machine should be replaced in the next financial cycle. He closed his laptop as a man knocked on his side window.

Boudro rolled down the window and the man asked, "You Boudro?"

"Yeah, what can I do for you?" He was used to people approaching him to repair their copy machines. People let their maintenance contracts expire and then asked Boudro to repair it for cash. It was a good side job for him, one the company did not allow.

The man said, "Enrique asked us to find you. He needs to talk to you."

Boudro was surprised a stranger knew he even knew Enrique much less knew he could track him down. Something wasn't right about this, he thought. "Enrique, who?" he asked.

"Your buddy Enrique Fuentes. We hear you and he have been tight since grade school. So we figure you might know where he is. We're looking for him because we owe him some money and want to pay him."

"No, man I ain't seen Enrique in a couple years. We used to hang but I got married and got a kid and my old lady don't let me go to bars no more. No, I ain't seen Enrique in a while," Boudro said.

The man pulled his shirttails up revealing a pistol in his waistband and said, "Boudro, why don't you come with us."

Boudro looked at the gun and said, "Hey man, I don't know nothing about Enrique. I gotta go." Boudro reached for the ignition switch of his car.

The man pulled the gun, pointed at Boudro and said, "Take your hand off the keys or your kid is going to be an orphan, now get out and come with us."

In the Whitecap Motel Boudro tried to convince the two men that he didn't know where Enrique was. But once the beating started, it wasn't long before Boudro gave up his buddy. Between having several teeth punched out of his mouth, a left eye that was swollen shut and the threat of his daughter being raped, tortured and murdered in a violent way, Boudro told the men where Enrique was hiding. His confession might have saved his wife and daughter but it didn't save him from the rope tightened around his neck that took his life.

Chapter 32

"**A**mber have you heard anything from those guys from Indiana?" Mark asked into his cell phone. Mark and Amber had gotten into the habit of talking most mornings as she drove to work.

"No, but a sheriff's deputy came in yesterday to ask if I have heard from Enrique. He said he heard that Enrique and I used to date and he was checking it out."

"What did you tell him?" Mark asked.

"Nothing. I mean, I said we dated last year for a few weeks but it wasn't anything. He asked when I saw him last and I told them it had been weeks. He seemed to buy it, thanked me and left."

"It has been a while since those guys visited you and I was thinking that maybe they gave up or moved on. Neither of us have heard anything since," Amber said.

Mark responded, "Yeah, you may be right; possibly they gave up and left."

Amber added, "Maybe they got caught. Maybe the cops arrested them for the murders and they're in jail."

Mark joined in suggesting possibilities, "Or perhaps they found Chopper's treasure and left with it."

"Maybe." Amber was silent for a moment then said, "I wonder where Enrique is? I worry about him."

"Amber, did you ever think that possibly Enrique ran off with the treasure, that he killed Chopper, stole the treasure and took off?"

"Yeah, I guess it's a possibility, just not one I like to think about. I want to remember Enrique as the sweet guy who treated me good."

"Amber, don't sell yourself short. There is a great guy out there for you. I have to get writing, call me if you hear anything."

"Yeah, I will Mark. Keep in touch. You make my morning commute more bearable."

~ ~ ~

"Mark! Answer the phone! Damnit Mark!" Amber said into her cell phone. She waited for the tone and left a frantic message for Mark to call her as soon as possible.

Sherry and Mark were on the beach relaxing. Sherry was talking with their daughter, their daily conversation and Mark was proof reading his latest Lake of the Ozark murder.

Will stepped out the kitchen door of the resort where he washed dishes. He sat on a pile of shipping pallets stacked up next to the dumpster and watched a man and a woman in the parking lot. The guy was yelling and the woman just stood there her head down staring at the concrete crying. Will moved closer to hear the couple without them seeing him. The man was yelling that the woman was a worthless piece of shit, that he should never have married her that he could have done much better than her, and he kept calling her a bitch. When Will saw the man raise his hand and slap the woman across the side of the face, asking "How's that bitch?" Will decided ... "He's gotta die."

That night Will waited in the parking lot hoping the man would walk back out to the car. He was a patient killer, he silently sat in the bushes, brushing mosquitos from his arms and face until the man appeared. It was obvious the man was drunk by the way he walked and steadied himself against the driver's door trying to get his car keys from his pocket. Will ran towards the car and with all of his strength slammed into him. The man's head smashed against the roof of the Mustang causing a bloody gash in his forehead, then Will shoved the limp man into the car. Will forced the drunk across the console and rammed his head into the passenger side window leaving a grotesque bloody imprint of his face on the glass. Will jumped into the car fished the keys from the man's pocket and drove out of the parking lot.

He drove down a gravel road, switched off the headlights and stopped at a sign in front of a house advertising campfire wood. It was late and there were no lights on in the house. Near the road were bundles of eight split logs tied together with binder twine that were sold for $5.00 a bundle. Will walked around the car, opened the passenger side door, and looked at the man, comatose from too much alcohol and his head twice being bashed into the Mustang. Will grabbed the drunk under the armpits and dragged him out of the car. He arranged the man in a seated position leaning against the pile of logs and removed a log from the top bundle. Will raised the log and brought it down quickly on the guy's head. The body slumped down as life drained from the corpse. Will let go of the log and it remained imbedded in the man's skull. Will stepped *back and looked at the scene and decided it looked pretty good and left the log projecting from the man's skull then asked, "How's that, bitch?"*

Will got in the car looking with satisfaction at the scene he left for some unsuspecting camper stopping to buy a load of split logs for their evening's campfire. "I'll bet the "s'mores" will never taste the same," Will laughed to himself.

Sherry hung up from talking with Mandy and asked Mark, "Are you going up to the room before long?"

Mark knew that was Sherry's way of asking for something but was too tired or too lazy to go up and get it, "Yes, what do you want?" He had to pee anyway.

"Could you get me something cold to drink," Sherry asked.

Mark closed his notebook, clipped his pencil in the spiral ring and stood up. The sun had warmed the sand and he hopped from one foot to the other as he slid his feet in his flip flops. "What do you want to drink?"

"Surprise me," Sherry said and got up to talk to Karen, Sue and Diane, condo neighbors.

Mark walked up the stairs with his towel draped over his shoulders and his flip flops making a slapping sound on each step.

After a visit to the downstairs half bath he walked to the kitchen, opened the refrigerator looking for something cold to quench his wife's thirst. He poured himself an iced tea in a tall glass of ice and added a dash of rum. Then he got out the blender and mixed a pitcher of slushy strawberry daiquiris for the ladies on the beach. He carefully balanced his drink, a stack of plastic cups and the pitcher of slushy red liquid and headed out the door just as he heard his phone ring.

He backed into the condo, set his load down on the kitchen counter and followed the ringing to the living room. He hadn't realized he had left his phone in the room.

"Hello Amber!" Mark said into the phone, happy to hear from her.

"Mark, there was another dead body discovered this morning or last night!" Amber practically yelled into the phone.

"Whoa, whoa slow down. What body?" Mark asked.

"I heard from a friend who said he heard it from a Marathon cop that Boudro was found dead up in north Key Largo, not too far from the Ocean Reef Club main gate."

"Who, or what is a Boudro?" Mark asked half-jokingly.

"Boudro LaFramboise. He is Enrique's best friend. He was found dead. Someone murdered him! Oh shit, a customer just walked in, I'll call you back." Then she hung up.

Mark thought for a minute, then grabbed the drinks and his phone and headed down to the beach. With each step down to the parking lot Mark reviewed the deaths that could be attributed to Chopper finding sunken treasure. Well at least I think Chopper found treasure, I guess I am assuming he found something valuable, he corrected himself.

"Ladies, I come bearing gifts of liquid refreshment to sooth your parched palates." Mark poured equal amounts in each cup. Luckily, he brought extra cups since Debby, Peggy, and Kate had joined the group on the beach. As he handed out the cups he told them to help themselves, there was enough left for a refill."

Mark layed back on his lounge chair, opened his notebook to a clean page and wrote at the top of the page, "Dead Men of the Keys."

He began to write a synopsis of the men killed over that last few weeks.

Chopper- Owner operator of a marine salvage company- rumored to have found Spanish treasure- he was tortured- found tied to a sunken boat off of Marathon.

Roberto Fuentes - Found beaten and tortured near the old Nike missile launch site in North Key Largo- connection to Chopper unknown other than Roberto was a brother to Luis and uncle to Enrique who both worked for Chopper.

Luis Fuentes- Worked for Chopper- left the Keys for a while- unusual for him- died of natural causes- father of Enrique, brother to Roberto, worked for Chopper.

Tim Main- An underwater archaeologist with a specialty in Spanish coins- killed in an automobile accident outside my condo- witnesses say he was driving erratically- his wife said him driving recklessly was out of character for her husband- Was he being chased by someone? Maybe his death wasn't accidental. He was on his way to meet Roberto about silver coins.

Enrique Fuentes- Worked for Chopper- in a relationship with Amber- was in hiding, now missing.

Told Amber he was going to be rich someday. Did he run off with the treasure? Is he somewhere hiding? Has he been killed, but not found yet? Did he kill Chopper, Roberto, Main and Boudro?

Boudro LaFramboise- Enrique's friend- found dead- a coincidence? Need more information about Boudro and his relationship with the other dead men.

"Wait a minute," Mark said to himself. "Assuming this Boudro guy was killed by the same people who killed the rest of the guys, and since he was recently killed, then it indicates they haven't gotten to Enrique yet. They were probably torturing Boudro trying to find Enrique. So Enrique is probably still alive. Come on Amber, call me. I need more information about this Boudro guy."

Mark wrote himself questions to ask Amber; *"Who is Boudro? How close were Boudro and Enrique? Is his death in anyway connected with the other deaths? Could Boudro have anything to do with the treasure? Does Boudro even know Chopper?"*

Chapter 33

The men parked their black Explorer in the Dunkin Donuts parking lot, ordered three large coffees and a half a dozen donuts. From there they walked along the highway to the Tavernier Creek Bridge. The man with the bag of donuts was eating a bear claw while he waited for the early morning traffic to clear, then crossed the road. The man holding the cups of coffee in a pressed cardboard tray waited for donut man to reach the end of the bridge, then both men stepped over the guardrail and started down the steep incline on opposite sides of the highway towards the cardboard enclave beneath the roadway.

The men figured the man living below the bridge would still be sleeping at 5:30 am but still they tried to be as quiet as possible. They wanted the element of surprise on their side.

Coffee man lowered his torso to peek below the bridge. All he saw was the cardboard enclosure Boudro told them they would find. There wasn't anyone in sight, there wasn't any movement. He looked across to the other side of the bridge and saw the man holding the donuts shaking his head back and forth indicating he didn't see anyone either. Coffee man picked up a small piece of coral and tossed it towards the cardboard compound. The coral bounced off the cardboard and rolled down the incline and plunked in the water. Both men watched to see if anyone responded. Nothing. The men figured the brown cardboard box shelter was unoccupied but crept forward cautiously just in case Enrique was a deep sleeper. Donut man looked over the enclosure and saw the outline of a person wrapped up in a blue blanket. He put his hand up in a halt position to warn coffee man, then pointed down with a hand to the side of his head to relate to the other man that someone was sleeping in the shelter. Coffee man shook his head indicating he understood.

Donut man called out to the prone figure, "Good morning brother. I am from the Key Largo Homeless Outreach Program and I brought you something to eat."

The figure under the blanket didn't stir. Louder the man said, "Hey, wake up brother, I have breakfast for you." Still no movement. Donut man was thinking the person was either sleeping off a drunken night or maybe he was dead. He pushed a box aside to gain access to the figure under the blanket. With a foot he gently probed the figure, nothing. He reached down and quickly jerked the blanket back. There wasn't a person under it only a pile of clothes arranged to look like a body.

Enrique was afraid of someone finding him when he slept and set up the blanket covered clothes as a precaution against intruders. He actually slept in a large box off to the side. Through the slit in the end of the box he could see donut man approach and heard him speaking. The donuts offered sounded good to Enrique and the man sounded like one of those do-gooders from the church that stopped by now and then but Enrique could see the handle of a pistol sticking out of the waistband of the man's shorts. He was not making a delivery from the food pantry.

As he watched, Enrique saw the man look down towards the creek bank and he made his move. He quickly burst free of the box and ran in the other direction, away from the man offering donuts. But his path took him right into coffee man. Enrique didn't know there were two of them. The second man responded by throwing a cup of hot coffee in Enrique's face. Instinctively Enrique raised his hands to his burning face and eyes. As Enrique screamed in pain, the man grabbed him and threw him to the ground while donut man ran through the cardboard shelter and dove on top of Enrique. Enrique's eyes were burning and blurred and he couldn't mount much of a fight against an opponent he couldn't see. As donut man repeatedly punched him in the face, coffee man secured his hands. Enrique had been found.

Chapter 34

"**M**ark, its Amber. I've got to be quick, it's busy as hell here today. Anyway," Amber whispered in the phone, "Boudro LaFramboise and Enrique were very close, have been since elementary school. If Enrique turned to anyone for help it would have been Boudro."

"Amber, are you sure it was Boudro who was found dead? I haven't found anything on the internet about it," Mark said.

"Yes, Davina came in the store and told me and she heard it from a cop. I think they're screwing on the side. Anyway, I know Davina from the bar."

Mark jotted down notes as they spoke, a habit he carried over from his reporter days. "Do you know how Boudro died?"

"Yeah, Davina said he was beat up. Mark, he was murdered like the rest of them. Someone figured out that Boudro and Enrique were good friends and tortured him, probably trying to get to Enrique."

"Do you think Boudro knew where Enrique was?" Mark asked. "Did Boudro even have anything to tell them?"

"I don't know. All I know is that Boudro is dead and Enrique is missing."

"Amber I think it is time we go to the sheriff's office and tell them all we know."

"No way in hell am I going to talk to anyone," Amber said. "Got a customer. Gotta go."

"Amber, call me on your way home," Mark said but it was too late. Amber had hung up.

Chapter 35

Enrique sat in the back seat of the black Ford Explorer, his hands secured with a plastic zip tie with donut man sitting next to him holding a gun pressed against his ribcage while the other man drove. "Where is the silver you found?"

"I didn't find no silver," Enrique replied.

"Enrique, we know you and Chopper found some treasure and your uncle was going to stores in Marathon trying to sell it. So don't give us any shit that you don't know anything about silver coins. Now, where the fuck are the coins?"

"I don't know what you're talking about. Maybe Chopper found some shit. He was always talking about finding treasure but I didn't find anything." Enrique said thinking that if he stayed with the story that he didn't know anything maybe they would eventually give up and let him go.

The man in the back seat was growing impatient with Enrique's lack of response and said, "I don't want to have to hurt you, but I will if you don't tell us what we want to know." Then he hit Enrique in the side of the head with the butt of the pistol and a trail of blood began running down the left side of his face.

"Hey man, I don't know what you're talking about. I don't have any silver; I didn't find anything. Honest, I don't have nothing. Do you think I would be living under a bridge if I was rich?"

The man punched him in the side of the face. Considering the tight confines of the back seat the punch was just a glancing blow, still Enrique felt the impact and his head jerked sideways.

The man turned to the driver and said, "Let's go somewhere more private so I can convince Mr. Fuentes that he needs to tell us where the silver is."

In the small cottage they rented in Islamorada Enrique was tied to a kitchen chair, unconscious, his head slumped down on his chest. Blood ran from cuts on his face and knife slashes on his arms. Enrique passed out from the pain of the beating he endured and the fingers on his right hand that were twisted and broken. A cup of cold water thrown in his face brought Enrique back to his reality.

One of the men grabbed his right hand and held it secure while the other man grabbed his index finger and bent it back, the joint cracking, and Enrique crying out in pain. He struggled, trying to pull away but his strength was gone, his mind blurred, and his resolve depleted. He mumbled, "Wait, I'll tell you where the silver is."

"Okay, now you're coming to your senses. Where is the silver?"

"You will never find it. I hid it. I gotta take you to it."

"Bullshit! You're just pulling some crap, you're stalling," the man holding Enrique's middle finger said and began to force it backwards.

"No! No. Really, you won't find the treasure. It's hidden in the mangroves. No one will ever find it. I'm the only person who knows where it is. If you kill me, you'll never find it."

The man let go of Enrique's finger and asked, "Where is it?"

Looking up at the men through swollen eyes Enrique answered, "North Key Largo, off an old trail."

"What trail, where?"

"I don't know the name of it, I just know where to turn off 905 and then you take a couple of more turns and walk for a mile or so, and you're gonna need a shovel, its buried. See, you'll never find it without me."

The men walked to the cottage kitchenette. Enrique could see their reflection in the screen of the television. The man who did most of the beating was eating a donut, while the other man opened a beer. Enrique tried to hear what they were saying but they were whispering. He wondered if his story of where to find the silver was convincing. He hoped that if they took him into the mangroves he would have a chance to escape, to save his life.

The men returned to the living area where Enrique was secured to the chair. Wiping powered sugar from his lips with the back of his hand one of the men said, "Alright, you're going to lead us to the treasure. We'll leave when its dark."

"But I'm not sure I can find it in the dark," Enrique said, trying to buy time for his rapidly decreasing lifeline.

"Yeah, well, we're gonna leave here early in the morning when it is still dark and it will be getting light when we get up there. You had better be telling us the truth or you will be begging me to kill you when I get done with your sorry ass."

Chapter 36

Enrique was still tied to a chair in the middle of the living area of the small two room ocean side cottage. When his captors allowed him to use the bathroom he looked in the mirror and saw a hideous creature looking back. He had several cuts above his eyes, cheeks and lips all crusted over with dried blood, his left eye was red and puffy from the beating and his right was totally swollen shut. The left side of his lower lip was bloated twice its normal size, but what hurt the most were his broken and disjointed fingers.

His assailants fell asleep around 10:00 according to the clock on the microwave, probably from the 12 pack they consumed. Enrique was still awake. He tried to organize his thoughts, but it wasn't easy to concentrate, with the pain he was suffering in his hands and head. He figured he probably had a concussion and tried to remember when he got it. Maybe it was when he was tackled under the bridge and his head hit the concrete or when he was punched so hard his chair tipped over backwards and his head bounced off the floor. It didn't matter where or when it happened, what mattered was that if he didn't get medical attention soon he would probably die from his injuries.

Enrique thought: What am I going to do? I've got to get away from these guys somehow. Maybe when they take me out to get into the car I can make a run for it. He knew it wouldn't be easy to fight off two guys with his hands tied but he had no choice. He would either die from the beatings or they would kill him when they found out the treasure wasn't in North Key Largo where he claimed it would be.

Chapter 37

Mark got up early, as always. He went downstairs, turned on the coffee pot, and went out on the balcony. While the coffee brewed he opened the laptop to check the news. He was a creature of habit and this was his morning ritual. Of late, the ritual included a call from Amber as she drove to work. They usually talked about Enrique missing and the murders.

Yesterday, Amber complained that her kitchen sink was clogged up. She had called her landlord about it in the past but she said this time she was going to try to fix it herself. Because as she said, "Whenever he comes over he stares at my boobs, makes rude comments and makes me feel uncomfortable. So screw him, I'll just crawl under the house and open the trap and see what is clogging the pipe."

Mark asked, "Do you know what you're doing? I mean do you know anything about plumbing?"

"Oh, a little. I used to watch my papa. He could fix anything. Hey, a girl on her own in the Keys learns to be self-sufficient. I've got a wrench thingy and I watched the landlord do it last time. I should be all right. I'm going to do it tonight when I get back from work and I'll let you know tomorrow morning how it comes out. The worst part is going in the crawl space under the house with all the spiders and creepy crawlers."

Mark sipped his coffee and read an article about what the president had tweeted that morning while he waited for Amber to call and report on her plumbing repair.

Mark refilled his cup and checked the time: 7:55 and no call from Amber. She must be running late, he thought. I'm curious how she made out with her plumbing project. She is quite a girl; she's kind, smart, pretty and apparently resourceful if she can fix her own plumbing.

Mark finished his second cup of coffee and Amber had still not called. He checked to see if his phone was set on silent mode. The phone was fine, she just had not called.

When Mark heard the toilet flush upstairs, he got up to make Sherry her morning elixir of French vanilla and caffeine. Sherry made her appearance on the downstairs balcony, hair brushed but still looking fresh from the pillow.

"Hello, beautiful!" Mark said.

Sherry plopped down in her seat, grabbed the cup of coffee on the table next to her, and holding it with two hands said, "I need this."

"What's wrong, not feeling so chipper this morning?" Mark asked knowing full well that Sherry would be hungover this morning. The two pitchers of strawberry daiquiris on the beach led to a couple of Margaritas at sunset. He was pretty sure the rest of the ladies were probably feeling a little under the weather as well.

Sherry cradled her cup and stared aimlessly out at the water of Florida Bay. Mark checked his phone, still nothing from Amber. He went back to the laptop and began to read the last chapter he had written of his Lake of the Ozarks book, although his mind was on Amber. Halfway though the chapter he reached for his phone on the table and looked to see if he had missed a call.

"Expecting a call?" Sherry asked.

"No, well actually yes. Amber said she would call on her way to work. She was doing some plumbing last night and was going to let me know how it turned out."

"Why don't you just call her?" Sherry asked.

"Yeah, I should just call her instead of sitting here worrying," Mark said as he punched her preset contact.

Mark listened to the phone ring as Sherry said, "Oh God, the sun is bright." Amber didn't answer. Mark left a message asking for her to call him when she got a chance.

Mark and Sherry followed their usual routine and went to the condo beach. Sherry layed back on a lounge chair, sun glasses blocking the harsh sun from her eyes and Mark sat with his notebook and pencil at hand waiting for inspiration to strike. But in the heat of the Florida Keys sun inspiration was replaced with perspiration. Mark checked his phone every few minutes. Amber hadn't called. It wasn't like her not to call. Even if she didn't have time she usually left a message. Mark called her number again. Still no answer.

Thoughts began to swim around in Mark's over active imagination. He began to question himself: Had something happened to Amber? Could she have been abducted by the guys that visited her at the shop? Or maybe she is just too busy to call him back. Did I say something to offend her and she's upset with me?

Mark leaned back and closed his eyes. He thought better without any outside stimulus to distract him. Amber almost always calls on her way to work. Why hasn't she called today? Why hasn't she returned any of my calls?

After dinner at Dillon's Irish Pub, Sherry wanted to run into CVS. Mark knew why. They were out of Tylenol and her head still called for a dose. Mark stayed in the car and tried Amber's phone again. Her phone rang twice and a voice came on telling Mark that the voice mailbox for the number he was calling was full.

"Shit. What does that mean?" Mark asked himself aloud. "I mean I know what it means but what does it mean for Amber? Why hasn't she taken any of my calls or apparently anyone else's? I am getting concerned for Amber's safety, he thought. She almost always calls me on her way to work. She always returns my calls. And now her voice mailbox is full and I have no other way to contact her. I could drive to her house and look for her but I don't know where she lives. Maybe I should drive down to Marathon tomorrow and check at the Treasure Chest to see if she is alright?

Mark's thoughts were interrupted when Sherry opened the passenger's side door. "Where were you?" Sherry asked.

"I'm just really concerned about Amber. She isn't answering her calls and now her voice mailbox is full. It's just not like her; she is always quick to return calls. I am concerned that something might have happened to her."

"Mark, should you call the police? I mean if you think that something might have happened to her, you should call someone."

"I know; I've been thinking about it. But, what do I tell them? A girl is missing and she might be involved in the murders of the guys around here in the last few weeks? Sheriff's deputies will sweep down on me for not reporting what I knew and they might arrest me, and Amber for that matter, for obstructing an investigation. We didn't really obstruct an active investigation, we are more like a couple of amateur sleuths investigating a crime, but we did withhold evidence. They could detain us for that, well me anyway, Amber seems to have disappeared."

Mark went silent. That was the first time he had said out loud what was in the back of his mind ... Amber has disappeared. He began to run the possibilities over in his head: Amber could have been abducted and is being tortured to give up Enrique, the guys who went to the shop knew she used to date Enrique. Or maybe she played Mark for a fool by opening up to him and gaining his trust and then ran off with Enrique and the treasure. Or maybe Amber was simply busy and didn't have time to call Mark and everything was okay.

Mark hoped she was just too busy but feared the worst.

The next morning Mark still had not heard from Amber. No calls, no texts, no communications at all. When Sherry came down for her morning drink Mark suggested that they take a ride down to Marathon and check in with Amber at the store. Never one to turn down an opportunity to go shopping, Sherry quickly agreed and was ready in an hour and a half, which Mark thought was pretty good for her.

After the nearly hour drive in heavy traffic, Mark parked in front of the Sandal Factory and walked down to the Treasure Chest. He peeked into the window looking for Amber but couldn't see inside due to the sun reflecting off the glass. He pushed open the door and the little bell announced his arrival. An older gray haired, balding man stood behind the counter and said, "Welcome to the Treasure Chest, how can I help you?"

Mark walked to the display case separating him and the man and asked for Amber. The man said, "She no longer works here. Is there anything I can help you with?"

Mark replied, "Amber is an old family friend and I was just checking in on her."

"I can't help you with that. She didn't come into work yesterday and I haven't seen or heard from her since. Kids these days don't have a work ethic. They don't give a shit they just up and leave without giving any notice." The man became angrier the more he talked, "They come in begging for a job then they just up and leave. No consideration at all. If you see her you can tell her that since she didn't have the consideration to call in and tell me she was quitting she has forfeited her back pay. I'm keeping it for her inconsiderate behavior."

Mark thanked the man and backed out as he continued to berate the youth of America and blamed all of the ails of society on the past president. Mark opened the door and the bell announced his departure.

Mark walked to his car in the parking lot and said to himself: Now I am really worried about Amber. She wouldn't just not show up for work. She is more dependable than that. Something has happened to Amber.

Sitting in the air conditioning of his car, Mark tried to call Amber. He got the same recording that the voice mailbox was full. Amber would never be without her phone. Like she said once, she and her phone were physically attached. There is a problem and I'm very worried for her.

Sherry walked out of the shoe store with a couple of shopping bags hanging from her hands. She opened the passenger side door and climbed in. "I'm hungry. Where are we going to have lunch?"

Mark smiled at his wife and said, "I'd like to go to a place where locals hang out. A place called Smugglers."

Chapter 38

Mark was worried about Amber. It had been days since he last heard from her and that wasn't like Amber. Since they first met, they hadn't gone more than a day without talking. She always returned his calls, maybe a day or so late but she either texted or called back. Since she didn't show up at work, just quit going in, he was sure something bad had happened. She might have just got scared and ran from the Keys, but she would have called me and said goodbye, or left a phone number where she could be reached. But Mark was afraid she may be a victim of the same fate as Chopper, Roberto, Boudro and maybe Tim Main and Enrique.

While Sherry was still sleeping and Mark sat on the balcony sipping coffee, he couldn't concentrate on the book, all he could think about was Amber. Mark decided he had to go to the sheriff and report her as missing. He knew he might be putting himself in jeopardy since he hadn't told the police about anything he and Amber had discovered about the deaths and the possible treasure. He thought for a minute and said, "But, then what have we really discovered? I'm sure the police have made the connection between Chopper and Roberto. I know they are still looking for Enrique so they must think he is somehow involved with the murders and the authorities know about Boudro and by now they must know about his relationship with Enrique. I guess I haven't really withheld evidence. But the police probably don't know about Amber disappearing. I've got to tell them so they can look for her. I don't even know where she lives. They probably can find out and can go to her house and check it out."

Mark was so absorbed in thought he didn't hear Sherry get up so he didn't have her morning brew ready when she appeared on the balcony. "Good morning gorgeous," Mark said. "Sorry, I was deep in thought and didn't hear you get up. I'll go get your coffee."

Sherry smiled and said, "That's okay," she held out her mug and said, "I did it myself."

Sherry knew Amber's sudden disappearance was bothering Mark. He wasn't acting himself, he often stared out at the water in thought. She didn't bug him about not having her coffee ready as she sometimes playfully did. It was just one of those silly little things that married couples did. She really didn't expect Mark to wait on her but if he forgot it became a joke between them.

"I'm going to the Sheriff's office and report Amber missing," Mark said breaking the silence. "I am very concerned that something terrible has happened to her."

"That's a good idea," Sherry said. "You really need to find out what happened, why she left so abruptly."

After a call to the sheriff substation and a brief conversation, Mark retuned to the balcony.

"Well?" Sherry asked.

"I told whoever answered the phone that I wanted to talk to Deputy Radak about a missing person. They asked a couple of questions and told me the deputy would contact me," Mark replied. "Now I just have to wait until I hear back from them."

Chapter 39

The men awoke Enrique at 5:18 by slapping him in the face. "Come on, it's time to go." Still uncomfortably tied to the chair, Enrique slept very little. His face, head, fingers hurt and his legs were cramping. He had a new pain, one on his right side. He wondered if he had some broken ribs.

"I gotta pee," Enrique said from his chair.

"So go ahead and piss," one of the guys said.

"No! I don't want no pissy pants on my car seats. Let him pee."

The shorter of the two men untied the rope behind Enrique's back, freeing his hands while the other guy picked up a large kitchen knife and said, "Don't do anything stupid and get yourself hurt."

Enrique realized this was not his opportunity to escape, when he stood up and almost fell over. He had been tied in the same position for hours and his legs were cramped and stiff. He walked to the toilet with short hesitant steps. There was no way he could outrun these two guys in the shape he was in. He hoped another opportunity would present itself later, after he had time to stretch out.

It was still dark and the rest of the residents of the ocean side cottages were still asleep. No one would notice the two men from the Wild Iris Cottage who were walking to the parking lot with a third man whose hands were tied behind his back and whose face displayed the results of hours of beatings.

The black Ford Explorer quietly pulled out onto US1 heading north. Traffic was sparse at that time, only a few cars, a couple of buses taking people from the mainland to work at the resorts of the Keys and some semi-trucks with loads of beer and other supplies heading for Key West. Most of the traffic was going south. The Explorer pretty well had the northbound lanes to itself.

"Go the speed limit," the man holding a knife near Enrique's ribs said, "We don't want to get pulled over with this guy in the car. One look at his face and a cop would arrest us for sure."

"I'm going the speed limit. Dammit, don't tell me how to drive," the driver said.

"My, my a little grouchy are we?" the man in the back seat with Enrique said. "You'll feel better when we have our hands on the treasure. Just think what all that silver will buy ya. You can buy a different hooker each night and you won't have to beat off all the time," the man said laughing.

"Oh fuck you," the driver said turning back to give his partner the finger.

"Watch out!" the man screamed from the back seat. The driver turned forward just as their black Ford Explorer ran through the red light at the Kmart and smashed into the Monroe County Sheriff's car crossing US1. The Sheriff's car was struck in the left rear quarter sending it spinning in circles across the highway and the Explorer bounded off the sheriff's car and crashed into a sign advertising the Tradewinds Plaza.

The driver of the Explorer was pushing the air bag from his face and his partner in the back seat was crawling up from the floor. Enrique was sprawled out on the rear seat, the knife held at his ribs as a threat was now protruding from his right side. The deputy, with a gash above his left eye and probably a concussion, ran to the Explorer to check on the occupants. He looked at the driver who was shaken up but seemed okay and the man in the back seat looked like he might have a broken arm. Then he looked at Enrique, his face swollen and cut from the beating he endured and the knife protruding from his side. The deputy knew there was something wrong. He drew his weapon and ordered the men to get out of the car. He told them to sit on the curb near the car as he reached in to feel for a pulse on Enrique.

The sirens of the fire rescue truck and an ambulance racing towards them could be heard as another sheriff's car arrived and took over the situation. The deputy who was in the accident sat down in obvious pain.

As handcuffs were being placed on the man from the back seat he leaned over to the driver and said, "You fucking idiot!"

Chapter 40

Mark followed his normal routine and woke up early, made a pot of coffee, and sat on the balcony and opened up his computer to peruse the news. As the computer booted up Mark thought of what the deputy told him after he went to check out Amber's house.

Nothing looked out of place. Breakfast dishes were still in the sink, Amber's clothes were hanging in the closet, her checkbook was there, her tooth brush and other toiletries were still in the house. It looked as if she left and didn't take anything with her.

That's not good, Mark thought. If she left on her own she would have packed a suitcase, taken her toothbrush and checkbook. I don't think she left on her own.

Mark looked at the Detroit Free Press site and moved to the CNN page. Nothing held his attention, his mind was on Amber. Mark clicked on KeysNet.net to see what was happening locally. A man was arrested on Big Pine Key for trying to use a stolen credit card. A Key West woman was arrested for spousal abuse; she beat the hell out of her husband. But what caught Mark's eye was an automobile accident on US1 in Key Largo, not far from their condo. Mark clicked on the headline and began to read.

After the first paragraph Mark said aloud, "What a stupid ass. A guy runs a red light and smashes into a police car." But, when he continued to read the article it really caught his attention. There was one fatality, a Marathon man named Enrique Fuentes. "Holy shit! Enrique is dead!" the article didn't say too much more other than the driver and a passenger in the car that ran the light had been arrested.

Chapter 41

Mark checked the local newspapers first every morning to follow the story that was unfolding about Enrique and the two men who were arrested for his murder. The man who was driving the car pled to a manslaughter charge in return for confessing to the murders of Chopper Wirsbinski, Roberto Fuentes, Boudro LaFramboise and Enrique Fuentes. He told how he and the other man were hired by the owner of the Island Gems Jewelry to find the stash of silver coins Roberto was trying to sell.

It had been weeks since Mark had heard from Amber. Nothing about her came out in the newspapers no mention of a local girl missing. Mark talked to Deputy Radak who investigated Amber's disappearance. He said the two guys who were arrested for the deaths of Enrique and the other men said they didn't abduct Amber or harm her in any way. Mark didn't believe it. Amber would never have left without saying goodbye. She would have told Mark she was leaving and she would have taken her toothbrush. Mark hated the thought, but he was pretty sure Amber had been murdered just like all the others. Probably tortured until she gave up Enrique. She probably knew where Enrique was all along. He wondered when her tortured body would be found by some tourist kayaking in the shallows along the edge of the mangroves, or discovered being consumed by animals in Crocodile Lake National Wildlife Refuge." Mark was sure he would never see or hear from Amber again.

Chapter 42

Life went on for Mark and Sherry wintering in the Florida Keys. Sherry went to lunch with the ladies from the condo and spent hours talking to Mandy on the phone. Mark awoke early each morning and read newspapers online but he set aside his fictional book about a serial killer murdering people in Missouri's Lake of the Ozarks. There had been too much death and violence in his life. The torture and murders of Chopper, Roberto, Boudro and Enrique were of interest to him but Mark didn't personally know them. To Mark they were like characters in a book playing out before him. But the disappearance of Amber was very real. He knew her. He talked to her. He had an emotional relationship with her. He liked her.

Mark took Amber's disappearance and probable death very personal. It haunted him. He couldn't help but blame himself for her death. He wondered if he had gone to the police sooner would she still be okay. Had he insisted she get away from Enrique and leave the islands for a while things would be different and he wouldn't be mourning a friend. Perhaps, if he hadn't gone into the Treasure Chest selfishly seeking information about Spanish treasure in the first place, Amber would not be missing now and possibly dead.

Mark hadn't told Sherry, but he had a recurring nightmare of Amber being raped, tortured and viciously murdered in a number of horrific ways. He awoke in a sweat and often got out of bed, walked the condo until his heartbeat slowed and his blood pressure went back to normal. Mark knew it would be one of the questions that would haunt him for the rest of his life; what happened to Amber?

~ ~ ~

Mark was packing the car getting ready for their return trip to Michigan. Their four-month vacation in the Florida Keys had gone by quickly. He was anxious to get back to their home in Upper Michigan, to his lake where he loved to fish and didn't have to worry about sharks and didn't have to rinse salt water off his fishing gear each time he used it. But he also didn't want to leave the Keys. He didn't want to leave thinking Amber might return and look him up and didn't want to leave thinking that she could be lying dead somewhere with bugs, snakes and rats gnawing on her body.

Two nights before they were to start up I-75 for the three-day drive, the residents of the condo held a going away party for all the snowbirds heading north. The table on the second floor commons area was filled with salads, meat and cheese trays, crock pots of three different kinds of meatballs, dishes of cookies, trays of brownies and, of course, a homemade Key Lime pie. Phone numbers, email addresses and Facebook information was exchanged and promises to stay in touch and visit were made.

The next morning several of the condo group met to hug friends before they drove out of the parking lot. Mark and Sherry would be leaving early the following morning and the goodbye hugs and promises to stay in touch would be repeated. As they were climbing the stairs to have their morning coffee, a UPS truck pulled into the parking lot, parked in the handicap spot and a man clad in brown shirt and shorts jumped out of the truck carrying a package. The driver started up the stairway towards the second floor. The package looked heavy by the way he carried it so Mark thought he would save the guy some time and trouble and asked, "Who's it for? I can deliver it for you."

The driver looked at the top of the package and read, "Mark Daniels. Unit 228."

"That's me," Mark said surprised. He hadn't ordered anything. Mark took the brown cardboard box from the deliveryman.

"You'll need to sign here to signify acceptance," Mark was told as a small tablet was pushed towards him. Mark balanced the heavy package on his knee with one hand and signed with the other. "Thanks, have a good day," the deliveryman said as he descended the stairs.

"What is it?" Sherry asked.

"I don't know, but it is heavy."

"Who is it from?" she asked.

"I don't know, there isn't a return address," Mark said as he looked the package over.

Sherry never could stand an unopened box and said, "Let's go upstairs and open this and find out what's in it."

Mark set the box on the dining room table and looked at all sides. There was nothing that indicated where and whom it was from. He took a steak knife out of the drawer and careful sliced through the multiple layers of packing tape holding it closed. "Someone certainly didn't want this to open accidently."

Mark folded the box flaps back one at a time as Sherry peeked in. A white envelope was at the top of the package. The sender used a black marker to print on the envelope, "For Mark Daniels ONLY!"

"What the hell is this all about?" Mark said as he pulled the envelope from the box. He turned it over and inspected it, then looked back at the inscription on the front.

Mark picked up the knife again and slit the clear tape sealing the envelope closed. Inside was a single folded sheet of paper with a hand written message. With a quizzical expression he unfolded the piece of paper and looked it over.

Mark's face flushed and his eyes welled up. He took a deep breath as a tear trickled down his cheek. "She's alive." Mark visibly shaken said to Sherry, "It's from Amber. She's alive!"

Dear Mark,

I'm sorry I left without telling you but I was scared. People I knew and were dear to me were dead. I had to get out of town and not leave any trace of where I went. But now Enrique is dead and the murderers are behind bars so I thought it would be safe for me to reach out to you.

I don't know if you remember but I had a problem with my plumbing and was going to repair it myself. I had to go in the crawl space and turn the water off. When I opened the trapdoor to the crawl space I found seven five-gallon plastic pails that weren't there the last time I was under the house. I looked in the pails and found Enrique's treasure. Buckets full of silver coins! He apparently he hid it under my house when he was living there.

That night I loaded the pails into my car and took off. I drove up to the mainland to hide and to figure out what I should do. I wanted to call you for advice but I needed to make a clean break. After I read that Enrique was dead I figured the treasure was up for grabs so I grabbed it. I found a company to appraise the treasure and sold it for over four hundred and seventy thousand dollars.

The first thing I did was send Enrique's mother a portion of the treasure her son died for. I also made a donation to help the homeless in the Keys, because I remember how hard and humiliating it was when I had to live out of my car.

Mark, I want you to know that you mean more to me than I could ever express. You treated me like a lady, not some bimbo in a dead end life. You took time to talk to me, you listened to me and considered my opinion, you made me feel confident, you made me feel important, you made me feel good about me. You were the rock that supported me throughout all of the death we lived through, without you I couldn't have made it.

I am still worried that some other modern day pirates will come after me and the treasure so I have not included my new contact information. With the money I am starting my life over, I owe it to all of those who died chasing their dreams and I owe it to me. I changed my name and moved far from the Keys where no one knows me. Where I can be me and not *be looking over my shoulder thinking someone is stalking me for the treasure.*

Mark after all we lived through together you will forever be a part of my heart. You were there when I needed you. You kept me sane, it's because of you I'm still alive. I can never repay you for what you did for me but enclosed is a small reminder of me and our short but memorable time together. The experience was filled with death, violence, uncertainty, pain and suffering, but you were my bright spot, the lighthouse guiding me through the storm. I will forever be grateful.

Love,

A

PS: I am enrolled at a community college. I'm a 29-year-old freshman! Thanks for giving me the confidence to take this step.

Mark handed the letter to Sherry and reached for a tissue to wipe the tears flowing down his cheeks.

"She's alive. She's alive and doing well," he said quietly as he looked in the box. Inside was another box taped at the seams. Mark reached in and withdrew it. It was a common brown box without any markings, heavy for its size. He used the knife to open it. He looked inside, smiled then reached in and lifted out a black, sea encrusted mass of silver coins.

Mark held it high and inspected it from all angles. In the six-inch-wide by four-inch-thick mass nearly a foot long there were the unmistakable shape of coins. Mark went out to the balcony to see his gift from Amber in the sunlight.

He sat in his chair on the balcony holding the black encrusted mass, thinking of what he and Amber had been through, about the men who died in their quest of this treasure; Chopper, Roberto, Tim Main, Boudro and Enrique. Sherry appeared bringing him a cup of coffee for a change, and asked, "What do you think of your piece of the treasure?"

"I wish I knew the history of the silver. Like, what ship is it from; is it riches from a Spanish treasure ship or plunder from a marauding pirate? How did the ship end up on the bottom, did it run around on the reef or as so many others, was a victim of a storm? And how many hands has the silver passed through and how many of the people died in pursuit of it? There are so many unanswered questions."

Thank you for reading.

Please review this book. Reviews help others find Absolutely Amazing eBooks and inspire us to keep providing these marvelous tales.

If you would like to be put on our email list to receive updates on new releases, contests, and promotions, please go to AbsolutelyAmazingEbooks.com and sign up.

About the Author

Wayne "Skip" Kadar writes fictional pieces under the name Justin Maxwell so as not to muddy the waters for readers of his non-fiction Great Lakes regional books.

Skip taught at the high school level for several years then became a high school principal. After 16 years a principal he retired from education. In retirement he worked as a harbor master at a marina on the Great Lakes and researched and wrote ten historically factual books about the Great Lakes region; books about ships that now lie on the bottom of the freshwater seas. He also writes about notorious criminals from the region.

Now fully retired, Skip spends time with his wife, Karen, at the family cottage outside Manistique, in Michigan's beautiful Upper Peninsula, at their home in Harbor Beach, Michigan on Lake Huron and winters in the fabulous Florida Keys.

ABSOLUTELY AMA⚡ING eBOOKS

AbsolutelyAmazingEbooks.com

or AA-eBooks.com

www.ingramcontent.com/pod-product-compliance
Lightning Source LLC
Chambersburg PA
CBHW050402030726
47503CB00006B/1977